Withdrawn

OTHER YA NOVELS BY HEATHER SMITH

The Agony of Bun O'Keefe
Baygirl (Orca)

CHICKEN

GIRL

Life can be a tough egg to crack

HEATHER
SMITH

PENGUIN TEEN
an imprint of Penguin Random House Canada Young Readers,
a Penguin Random House Company

First published 2019

1 2 3 4 5 6 7 8 9 10

Jacket illustration and design by Jennifer Griffiths

Manufactured in Canada

Library and Archives Canada Cataloguing in Publication

Smith, Heather, 1968-, author
Chicken girl / Heather T. Smith.

Issued in print and electronic formats.
ISBN 978-0-14-319868-0 (hardcover).—ISBN 978-0-14-319869-7 (EPUB)

I. Title.

PS8637.M5623C55 2019   jC813'.6   C2018-900742-7
                                            C2018-900743-5

Library of Congress Control Number: 2018936947

www.penguinrandomhouse.ca

Penguin
Random House
PENGUIN TEEN CANADA

To Rosie, who makes my heart swell.
And, always, to Rob.

CHAPTER ONE

I had one leg in the feathery yellow costume my boss called a uniform when Cam stomped into my room like a runway model on crack and thrust his chest out at the end of my bed.

"Pops? Be honest. Do I have"—he paused for effect—"moobs?"

It was a running gag, our use of word blends. He was obviously trying to one-up me after I'd used *automagically* earlier that day.

"Nice try," I said. "But if it doesn't fit organically into a conversation it doesn't count."

He looked down at his torso. "If you must know, the development of man boobs are a genuine concern of mine."

I gave his naturally athletic body a once-over. "Pfssh. Yeah, right."

I stepped into the other leg of my costume. "Now, if you'll excuse me. I'm running late and don't have time for this meaningless"—I paused for effect—"nonversation."

He groaned in defeat. "Damn you, Poppy."

I was almost out the door when he said, "Pops?"

I turned around. "Yeah?"

"I love seeing you happy."

And just like that, the smile fell from my face.

"What's wrong, Pops?"

My sweet Cam. Didn't he know? Happiness was only temporary.

I put on my head. "I'm fine. I'm late, that's all."

It was true.

I only had ten minutes before I had to be curbside holding a sign: *Hot and spicy chicken wings, $8.99 a dozen.*

⤙

I walked down Churchill Street identifying each house as I passed: Plan 47-17, Plan 47-28, Plan 47-6. I'd been obsessed with wartime houses ever since I'd found the blueprints in the basement when I was ten. Each design was outlined in an affordable housing pamphlet for returning vets. Discovering that I lived in a home built during the war sent my imagination soaring. I became obsessed not only with wartime housing but with the whole era. It made me feel a longing, for what I didn't know. Simpler times, maybe. I figured everyone was happier in the forties.

I followed the railway tracks into the downtown core. If I kept walking I'd reach the nicer part of downtown and eventually my school, but I stopped smack-dab in the middle of Elgin Street, where the surroundings were run-down and shabby. One building stood out though: Chen Chicken. Its white fairy lights twinkled all year round and the crisp white storefront looked warm and inviting.

I snuck in the back door and grabbed my sign. I was ten minutes late. With any luck Mr. Chen would think I had been there all along.

I walked up and down Elgin doing my usual moves— the hop, the skip, the jump. The sweat rolled off me. It wasn't the best summer job in the world but it was nice to be someone else for a change. Even if that someone was a bird.

I held the sign skyward, gave it a shake. A drunk walked up to me, said he wanted to cluck me. I said, "Selfies and high fives only." I wasn't about to engage in interspecies sex for ten dollars an hour, that was for cluckin' sure.

Mr. Chen yelled from the shop. "Work harder, Poppy Flower!"

I didn't hate the nickname. It was kind of clever . . . Poppy Bauer, Poppy Flower. What I hated was having it yelled at me ten times a day.

I did a violent 360-degree spin and cocked my head as if to say, *Happy now, old man?*

He wobbled his hand back and forth. I'd never be more than a so-so.

When he went inside I tried grapevining. Not easy with giant chicken toes. Especially with that thing sticking out the back. What even is that? Another toe pointing backwards? Jesus, chickens were weird. And I was one of them.

A little girl appeared in front of me. She was a beautiful mix of pattern and color. Her yellow sundress was covered in cat faces and her backpack was dotted *and* striped. She wore her hair in two braided buns, high on her head like mouse ears.

I stood up and wiggled my hips to dislodge my last-resort underwear, the thong I'd bought because *Vogue* said they were in. *In*. Ha ha.

The little girl clapped her hands four times. I'd worked in a chicken costume long enough to know why.

"I wasn't doing the Birdie Dance," I said. "It was my underwear. It was kind of stuck."

The way her face fell—this wasn't her first disappointment and it wouldn't be the last.

"Sorry," I said. "That song, I'm mocked with it like ten times a day."

She smiled as if she understood. "I get it."

She wrapped her fingers around her backpack straps. "Well, bye."

I watched her walk down the road. Halfway down, she sat on the curb. She reached into her backpack and pulled out a stuffed toy. She wrapped her hand around one of its long ears and popped her thumb in her mouth. She wasn't doing it on purpose, but she was pulling my heartstrings, plucking and playing them like a maestro. I waddled toward her and put down my sign. When she looked up, I formed beaks with the tips of my wings. A smile formed around her thumb.

I cleared my throat.

"*Da-da-da-da-da-da-da . . .*"

We did the whole song, even the skipping in a circle bit. When we were done she said, "You're a really nice chicken."

I felt my spirits lifting. All because a random child told me I was nice. *Go on, spirits,* I thought, *sink. You'll only get pulled down anyway.*

"My name's Miracle," she said. "And this is Gilbert."

I shook her rabbit's paw. "Nice to meet you, Gilbert."

I picked up my sign and got back to work. Miracle walked alongside me.

"Miracle," I said. "Why are you out all by yourself?"

She linked her arm around my wing. "Why are you so yellow?"

"Because chickens are yellow," I said.

She looked up. "Are they?"

I pictured one in my head. It was brown.

"Actually, now that I think of it, maybe not."

"Maybe you're a chick," she said.

"Seriously though," I said, "aren't you too little to be out on your own?"

"Little?" she said. "I'm six!"

When she talked to me, she looked up into the costume's face—not mine, which was hidden behind a mesh screen in the chicken's neck.

I stopped walking and crouched down. "I'm right here, you know."

She squinted through the sheer material. "Oooh, you're pretty."

I steeled myself. *Stay where you are, spirits.*

"What's your name?" she asked.

"Poppy."

"How old are you, Poppy?"

"Ten years older than you."

She counted on her fingers.

"You're forty-two?"

I laughed. "Sixteen."

"So you're in eleventh grade," she said. "Like Lewis."

"Who's Lewis?" I asked.

"He's my very best pal."

She reached up, stroked my feathers as if I were a real live animal.

"Tomorrow's the last day of school," she said. "We're having cake. I voted for vanilla but chocolate won."

"That's too bad," I said. "They should compromise and get marble."

She ran her fingers across the feathers on my shoulder. "You're smart, Poppy. I'm going to tell Thumper all about you."

I bent forward so she could pet my head. "Who's Thumper?"

"Thumper's my friend," she said. "He's one hundred years old. He lives under the Fifth Street bridge."

"You've been under the Fifth Street bridge?"

"I'm there every night."

Any more pulling and my heartstrings would snap.

I straightened up and we continued walking.

"You should come," she said. "You could meet Buck. He talks funny. He says it's because he's from across the pond. You could meet Lewis too. He takes care of me. His head is shaved on the sides. It feels like stubble. You know, like when a man forgets to shave? My dad had stubble all over his head. He was in the army. But then he died."

She waved her arms around a lot when she talked. Her lips moved around a lot too. Probably because her tongue was busy navigating the toothy gaps that filled her mouth. She wore Mary Jane shoes with lights in the soles. Her socks were red with white polka dots. Everything about her made my heart feel achy. I wasn't sure why.

She stopped walking and turned to face me. "So, will you come?"

There was something heartbreaking about the way she lisped the word *so*.

I didn't want to hurt her feelings so I answered with a maybe.

But for the rest of the day they sat in the back of my mind—the girl, her rabbit, and her polka-dotted socks.

The best thing about going to work was coming home to Plan 47-24. It was, in my opinion, the best of the wartime home designs. My favorite part was the upstairs. There were just two rooms, one on the left, one on the right—one for me, one for Cam. Our slanted ceilings made things extra cozy.

It was 7:45. My parents would be watching *Coronation Street*. It was the same every night—while they filled their heads with the fictitious lives of working-class Brits, I filled my head with darkness.

It was what I did now.

Our living room was small and sparsely decorated. Even though there were two leather recliners, my parents chose to curl up together on the old, lumpy couch. It wasn't long ago that I'd have joined them, making room for myself by squishing my healthy-sized butt between them. I had stopped doing that. It was too risky. I was getting bad at faking it and I didn't want them to see the clues. They'd only blame themselves for my sadness. And they had nothing to do with it.

I said a quick hi and went upstairs. Within minutes I was in my sweats, looking at The Photo. I read the comments. Twice. Then, as I always did, I looked for evidence that it wasn't just me, that there had been other victims as well. It was meant to be helpful, knowing that I wasn't alone, but it only made me more miserable.

It didn't stop me from searching though.

There was this one photo of a baby born with birth defects. His skull was larger than average and his eyes drooped. Someone had taken his photo from a fundraising page and captioned it: *That face you make when your parents are actually cousins.*

The Photo seemed lame in comparison.

But that wasn't the point.

The point was, the world is a cruel place. I knew that now.

The Photo changed me. It opened up a portal into wickedness and I jumped in with two feet.

I clicked from one horrible video to another. I was watching a boy being beaten up for carrying a purse when

Cam barged in. He stood in front of my mirror with his hands on his hips, giving himself a good once-over. He had legs for days, even more so in his denim shorts. He nodded toward the floor. "What do you think?"

I looked down. He was wearing the most sparkly silver heels I'd ever seen.

"They're quite"—I paused for effect—"fantabulous."

He groaned. "Lame."

"Okay, then," I said. "They're quite"—I paused longer for even more effect—"craptacular."

He laughed. "I'm thinking of wearing these when I emcee the assembly tomorrow."

It was supposed to be the two of us up there, our final double act of the year. We'd been practicing for months.

I burst out crying.

"Oh, Pops."

He sat on the bed and wrapped his arms around me. He'd overdone it on the cologne, but I sobbed into his designer shirt anyway. It must have been killing him but he let me soak it—further proof he was the greatest brother on earth.

I sat up and wiped my eyes. "I'm sorry," I said. "I'm just a bit jealous, that's all."

He smiled. "Don't worry. You can borrow my craptacular shoes anytime you like."

I snorted with laughter.

"Don't do that, Pops," he said. "It's very unbecoming."

I wiped my nose with the back of my hand. "Being female doesn't make me a delicate little flower, you know."

"Don't worry, Pops. No one would ever describe you as delicate."

He slipped off his shoes and stretched out on the bed. "You know, you can still join me on stage tomorrow. There's still time."

I filled the space beside him and stared at the ceiling. "No thanks. I've had enough of the limelight."

He turned to me. "You're not still looking at that stupid photo, are you?"

"Pfssh. No."

He raised an eyebrow.

I sighed. "It's like I've been poisoned. I see sadness in everything now."

He stared at me for a minute, then said, "Russian dolls. They're so full of themselves."

I laughed. "What was that?"

He smiled. "Me being your antidote to sadness."

He reached out, wrapped his pinkie around mine. "Remember how we used to fall asleep like this?"

I liked it back then, when life was simple.

"Yeah," I said. "I remember."

"Do you remember our very first pinkie promise?"

"No."

"It was in the womb."

"No it wasn't."

"Yes it was," he said. "I remember it clearly. I punched through my amniotic sac and into yours and I grabbed your teeny-tiny baby finger and promised to love you forever."

I almost believed him. Cam was born a fighter. He'd been in boxing lessons since he was three. In fourth grade he'd threatened a kid for stealing my granola bar. He said, "Still hungry? Here, have a knuckle sandwich." He was suspended for a week.

I rolled on my side. He had a gorgeous face. Gorgeous skin, high cheekbones. He knew how to work it too. Brows plucked perfectly, a touch of liner under the eyes, hair dyed a golden blond. A friggin' goddess.

"I met a little girl today," I said. "She wore Mary Jane shoes with lights in the sole and red-and-white polka-dot socks."

His eyes followed mine to the Rosie the Riveter poster that hung on my wall.

Rosie used to make me think I could do anything.

Then I found out that I couldn't.

⚞

Cam had bought me the Rosie poster for our eleventh birthday. I loved how badass she looked in her iconic polka-dotted bandana and denim coveralls. The best part was the way she flexed her right bicep. The "We Can Do It!" in the speech bubble above her head was the icing on the cake.

The campaign would have worked on me, had I been alive in the forties. I'd have marched out of my traditional role in the home and joined the workforce, replacing the men who were fighting overseas. I'd have been a pioneer.

When I was twelve, I dressed as Rosie the Riveter for Halloween. I even went to Canadian Tire and bought a rivet gun. I told the treat-givers that I was going to build airplanes someday. Or ships, or tanks. I got some funny looks . . . and some extra candy. I adopted the red-and-white polka-dotted bandana into my regular style after that. Soon after came the thrift-store shopping. I'd mix vintage with modern—pleated A-line skirts with Doc Martens, red peep-toe shoes with ripped cut-offs. All looks would be finished off with a touch of bright red lipstick.

Then, six months ago, The Photo appeared, and slowly I slipped away. Cam would say, "Stop sucking in, Pops, for God's sake. You're going to cause internal organ damage." I'd let the body shaming get to me. I had thought I was stronger than that.

In ninth grade, the captain of the girls' rugby team said I should try out for the team because I was built like a brick shithouse. I loved that description. It was so much better than "big-boned," which was how my mother described me. I was welcomed to my first (and last) rugby practice with open arms. A particularly vocal girl told me she was impressed by my tree-trunk legs and linebacker shoulders. I made sure she was the recipient of my very first tackle. When I landed on top of her she poked me deep in the belly and said, "Wow, you're, like, all flab on the outside but your core is rock hard." In the change room, while I stood in my bra and underwear, she shared her findings with the rest of the team. They laughed and told me not to mind Eve, she was born with no filter. The next day, she plunked herself next to me in the lunchroom. With more freckles than face and a head of wild copper hair, she was striking to look at. She said, "I was up all night thinking about what's soft on the outside but hard on the inside, but I could only think of examples for the other way around—turtles, eggs, a human head. But then I closed my eyes and remembered my fingers sinking into your gut and reaching your kick-ass abs and then I finally came up with one." She didn't tell me what it was—she showed me photos of her roller derby team instead. She nodded at my headband and said, "It was a popular sport in the forties. You'd fit right in." Then she stood up and said, "See ya, Peach."

I tightened my abs and smiled. *Peach*. I liked that.

It made perfect sense that roller derby would be big in the forties. Women were really coming into their own back then and strong, curvy bodies were the trend. I would have been right at home. Admittedly, I was a little bit more than curvy. But I did have the desirable hourglass shape of the era. In fact, mine was even better—instead of being made from hard, breakable glass, it was as soft and as squishy as a luxury feather pillow.

I liked Eve. She was blunt, but she was honest and she had good instincts. She was right about derby—I did fit in. I became a valuable part of the team, thanks in big part to my build. I was lucky. Most people were either slim, chubby, fat, or obese. But I was an hourglass-shaped brick shithouse with the softness of feathers. My only problem was, that strong inner core didn't show in photos.

One night, about four a.m., Cam barged into my room. He'd gotten up to go to the bathroom and saw the light on under my door. Tears streamed down my face. I said, "I've been trying to close my laptop for hours now." He closed it for me. He said, "Those comments are garbage."

"Yes," I said. "And garbage never goes away. Just look at the landfills."

He didn't have a response to that. He just hugged me. I breathed in the springtime scent of his pajama shirt. It was a nice change from the stench that was constantly under my nose.

He said, "Things aren't as bad as they seem, Pops."

I laughed. "That's easy to say when you're on the outside looking in."

His face fell. "Outside looking in? We're twins, Pops. I'm on the inside with you, looking out. Always."

Part of me wished it was true. I'd like to have company in the dark. But Cam didn't belong on the inside with me. He deserved to be free.

The struggle to keep away from the filth was almost as troubling as the filth itself. In the end it was easier to let go, to immerse myself in it, to roll over and say, *Yes, yes. You're right. Look at me. Who did I think I was, believing in myself?*

I hung up my bandana, waved it like a white flag.

I traded my lipstick for Chapstick. The original kind. I didn't deserve cherry. The only thing I deserved was liposuction or death.

I became a faded version of myself.

I was like a Polaroid left out in the sun.

The problem with school was that it was a bit of a laugh. Cam and I were the dynamic duo known for entertaining the students and teachers alike. But what came easy before—the jokes, the witty repartee—was becoming harder to deliver. Any humor I could muster came out flat so I avoided it altogether. The school library became my fortress and the books that I pretended to read were my armor. It was boring as hell but I knew it was better than sitting home watching horrific crap on the internet.

Mom knocked on my door. "You're going to be late, Poppy."

I was glad school was almost over but I'd miss the structure—if I didn't get up for school, I mightn't get up at all. At least I had my daily four o'clock supper shift at Chen Chicken to look forward to.

God, I was pathetic.

I got out of bed and pulled a brush through my hair. Cam's voice floated from his room to mine. He was rehearsing his lines. I tossed the brush on my dresser and got back in bed. I sunk deep down under the covers and convinced myself I was doing it for Cam. My absence on the stage would be easier to explain if I was absent from school.

A few minutes later, my door swung open.

"Poppy! Didn't you hear me calling? You're going to be late."

I curled up and held my stomach. "I've got cramps. They're killing me."

Her face softened. "Aw, that's too bad. You'll be missing the very last day."

I played along. "Yeah, bummer."

I must have been wearing a convincing *my uterus is killing me* face because later, at lunchtime, she came back with a bottle of ginger ale, a bag of popcorn, and a bucketload of sympathy. "I thought we could watch a movie together."

It was like offering a drink to an alcoholic. I would have loved to gobble down Mom's offer—but I'd have only been left riddled with guilt. There was a cloud over me now. Whenever nice things happened it darkened. It was a reminder—*I* may have been having a jolly old time but somewhere there was somebody who wasn't.

"Sorry," I said, throwing back the covers. "I told Cam I'd come in if the Advil kicked in."

Her face fell.

I gathered my clothes. I wouldn't change in front of her.

As I passed her on my way to the bathroom I said, "Another time, okay? We have all summer, right?"

She smiled. "Of course. Have fun at the assembly."

I sat on the edge of the tub, waiting for her shadow to pass across the crack at the bottom of the door. I'd left her cold, feet frozen to the floor, staring at the emptiness of the space I'd filled moments before.

What she didn't know was that the emptiness had been there all along.

It had been in the shape of an hourglass.

Ralph Donaldson was sitting on a plastic lawn chair in front of Plan 47-4.

Frank Rogers was trimming his hedge outside Plan 47-14.

They were talking loudly about the weather. Frank figured it was hot enough to fry an egg on the sidewalk. Ralph said he'd watched a science program on the CBC and the experts had concluded that it was unlikely—that the egg would cook unevenly, if at all, and that a better choice would be to fry the egg on the hood of a car because metal is a better conductor than concrete. Frank said he'd be tempted to give it a try but didn't want to waste a good egg. Frank and Ralph pronounced *egg* as "aig." When Frank saw me approaching he said, "Here's someone who should be an expert on the subject."

I laughed. "Is that all you see me as now? A chicken? I'm not even in costume."

He looked at his watch. "You will be at a quarter to four. I figure even part-time chickens must be experts on aigs."

I leaned against the picket fence at the end of his lawn. "To be honest," I said, "the only thing I know about aigs is that they really hate Fry-days."

Frank didn't get it. Ralph explained. "Friday but with a *y*?"

Frank laughed. "Good one, Poppy."

I could have stayed there all afternoon, talking about the weather and making corny jokes about aigs. I liked Frank and Ralph. They'd both had me in their houses to look at their four-bedroom layouts (ours was only three). Frank's bedroom and living room were in the front, while his kitchen/dining room and second bedroom were in the back. Ralph, on the other hand, had his kitchen/dining room in the front, adjacent to his living room, and in the back were both his first and second bedrooms. Every room was just the right size. Both had the charming sloped-ceiling top floor with two bed-rooms side by side.

I went to a party in the suburbs once. At Eve's cousin's house. From the front door I could see the kitchen, living room, and dining area. A spiral staircase wound its way to a balcony that I assumed led to a multitude of bedrooms. *What this house needs*, I thought, *is walls.*

The houses in my neighborhood were full of them. Every room had four and being enclosed within them felt cozy and safe.

I said goodbye to Frank and Ralph and continued on to school. When I passed the chicken shop I stopped and squinted through the window. Mr. Chen was in the back, lowering a bucket of soapy water from the sink to the floor. I figured a friendly wave might improve our relationship so I knocked—*Tum-ti-ti-tum-tum. Tum-tum!* He jumped a mile and dropped his bucket. We watched, he from the kitchen and me from the window, as soapy water flooded the floor. Eventually he looked up. When he did, I waved. He wasn't impressed.

I continued down Elgin, crossed the even grungier James Street, and eventually turned onto Queen, which was full of bistros, bakeries, and bookshops. I felt an urge to knock on the windows. The occupants would drop their breakfasts, breads, and books and I'd run off, leaving chaos and confusion behind. I'd become the notorious neighborhood knocker. There'd be community meetings about how to stop me. People would pull together. The owner of the Friendly Bean would meet the owner of Sweetie Pies and together, with the owner of Turn the Page, they'd form a neighborhood watch. They'd become a tight-knit community. And even though I'd eventually get caught, the relationships between the residents would remain strong because of what they'd been through. They'd be the Home Front and I'd be the War, and when it was over they'd all be better for it.

I turned off Queen and looked to the sky. I imagined a bomb dropping and wondered if the person who posted The Photo would run into the streets to help or cower under their computer.

I thought I knew the answer.

My school appeared in the distance. Another faded Polaroid. I walked into the pale-pink brick building grateful it was the last day, hoping that any final good moments wouldn't cloud my judgment. I wouldn't want to be duped into a false sense of security.

The assembly was just starting. Cam was surrounded by the usual gaggle of girls. He called them his Cam-elles. I called them the Drome-drearies. Cam didn't get it until I said, "You know? Dromedary? As in Arabian camel?" He said, "What do you call a camel with no humps?" and when I said, "A horse?" he said, "No, Humphrey!"

Cam was my antidote to everything.

When Cam came out of the closet, the Cam-elles came out of the woodwork. They loved their little gay mascot. Cam couldn't see it, but he was being defined by his sexuality. It's like how gay characters on TV can't just happen to be gay—their homosexuality has to be part of some comedic shtick. Like that's all they're about as human beings. I asked Cam if he even liked these girls. He said he liked the attention. At least he was honest.

Cam came out at the beginning of ninth grade. A few months later, I found his boxing gloves in the trash. I told him he was becoming one-dimensional. He said, "Why? Because I don't like butch sports anymore?"

I said, "Don't you know, Cam? You can be the boxing king *and* the eyeliner queen, all at once."

My sweet Cam. He'd come out of the closet only to squish himself into a box. I hated that.

The assembly started. Cam was rocking his heels and rocking the mic. He looked gorgeous. But then he always had a way with makeup, even as a little kid. I loved that side of him.

I loved *all* sides of him.

Eve found me sitting in the back row of bleachers. "I wish you wouldn't hide from me."

"Me? Hiding? Pfssh. I'm not hiding."

She sat down beside me. "I hate your jeans."

They were boyfriend cut, loose fit with rips at the knees.

"You have the same pair," I said. "I've seen you wear them."

"Yeah," she said. "But they suit me. These don't suit you."

I knew what she was getting at but chose not to respond.

"I was in Value Village last week," she said. "There was this dress—you would have loved it. It had puffed sleeves and it went in tight at the waist and the skirt part was really big."

I kept my attention on the jazz band, who were killing "Fly Me to the Moon"—and not in a good way.

Eve talked over them.

"Last week, after we beat the Killbillies, I tweeted a photo of the team looking all badass and victorious, and before I knew it there were a hundred strangers commenting about how derby girls were a bunch of man-hating dykes."

I made a mental note to find the thread and strangle myself with it.

She pulled a Jolly Rancher out of her pocket, green apple to match her freshly dyed hair.

"Some people around here have been wondering how one stupid photo made you lose your mind," she said. "But I get it. It's not the photo or what was said about it, it's that nastiness is the norm."

Her perceptiveness was why I'd been hiding from her. If she kept identifying my problems, I'd be expected to work through them, and I wasn't nearly done wallowing.

"In the Mood" blared from the stage. If I'd been wearing the Value Village dress I could have jitterbugged to it. God knows I'd watched enough instructional videos.

The Jolly Rancher clickity-clacked in Eve's teeth.

"Don't you miss it?" she said. "I'd die without derby."

Eve was a jammer. Her job was to skate through a pack of blockers. I was the pivot—a special blocker who could become a jammer during the course of play. I had the best of both worlds. I got to lead my team in blocking the other team's jammer but I also had the opportunity to score whenever Eve passed me her helmet cover with the special star designation. Would I die without derby? Obviously not. But I did miss it.

She popped another candy in her mouth and offered me a blue raspberry one. I put it in my pocket.

"Just so you know," I said, "I haven't lost my mind."

She swept her shoulder-length hair to the side, revealing a sleek razed undercut. "You sure?"

I took no notice of her. Her skate name might have been Poison Evie but there was nothing toxic about her at all.

"There's a new girl on the team," she said. "She's good, but she's no Rosie the Pivoter."

I took the Jolly Rancher out of my pocket and slipped it in my mouth. It was all at once sweet and sour.

"Guess what?" she said.

"What?"

"I work at the arena now. At the concession stand. You should come for a skate sometime. I'll give you a free slushie when Eddie's not around."

The last time I had been skating was almost five months before. I had spent the whole time feeling unsettled because I didn't know if I was having fun or not. It's like when you're feeling nauseous and you're not sure if it's because you're hungry or because you're sick. It'd be easier if you were throwing your guts up because at least then you'd know for sure. That's why I started wallowing—because being miserable when you're wallowing is way easier than being miserable while you're having fun.

I inched away from Eve and nodded to the stage. "Cam's coming back on."

He worked the stage like a pro but he was playing up his sexuality, cracking jokes at his own expense. He had his own comedic shtick and I hated it.

Queen's "Don't Stop Me Now" blared from the speakers. Cam was known for nailing lip-sync routines and this one was no exception. He was Mr. Fahrenheit alright. He was two hundred degrees of hot shit and the audience loved him. He was turning the world inside out, just like he always did, and when he was done burning through the sky he slid across the stage on his knees and collapsed in a dramatic heap. He stayed there until a good thirty seconds after the song ended, and the effect was staggering. When the cheering died down he hopped up and bowed. I felt proud until he said, "Just thought a little queen would brighten your day."

Eve leaned in. "That brother of yours is the total package."

I agreed. He was like a beautiful box tied up in ribbons and bows.

It was what was happening on the inside that I was worried about.

Instead of spending the rest of the school day in the library pretending to read like usual, I spent it hanging out with Eve, pretending I hadn't lost my mind. We went to the gym to watch a friendly teacher-student volleyball match, then ate some cake the principal was handing out in the lobby. It was chocolate.

When school was over, I walked home with Cam. He told me he missed me being on the stage but we both knew I couldn't have pulled off that much happiness.

When we got home, I put on my chicken suit. I liked looking at the world through chicken eyes. In a weird way, it suspended reality. Say, for example, one of the druggies from James Street stumbled up onto Elgin and collapsed in the middle of the sidewalk and died right in front of your eyes—well, when you're in a chicken costume you're not really there, you're just a pair of beady eyes under a pile of feathers. Not that any of that really happened. It could have, it's hard to say for sure. That's just one of the perks of being a chicken.

As I was leaving, Cam tweaked my beak. "This getup never gets old."

"If you like it so much, you should apply for the lunch-time shift," I said.

"This summer job thing," he said, "it's so below me."

"You're going to have to find something," I said.

"What I really want," he said, "is to become a"—he paused for effect—"celebutant."

"Like the Kardashians?" I said.

He nodded. "I want to be rich and famous for no good reason."

"Sounds good," I said. "But being rich and famous has its drawbacks. I mean, you wouldn't want to come down with a bad case of"—I paused for effect—"affluenza."

He groaned in defeat. "Damn you, Poppy."

⚒

Frank called to me from Ralph's lawn. "Hey, Poppy, how does a chicken tell the time?"

"I don't know," I said. "How?"

Frank elbowed Ralph. "Tell her, Ralph."

Ralph cleared his throat. "He looks at the cluck."

"Ha ha. Good one," I said.

Frank slapped his knees. Ralph wiped his eyes. I said goodbye and kept walking. I wondered how long they took to come up with their joint joke. Then again, what did it matter? They had all the time in the world.

He looks at the cluck.

I wondered if male was always their default.

Sometimes I wondered about their wives. What did *they* do all day? Cook? Clean? Do the laundry? I liked

Frank and Ralph but wondered what gave *them* the luxury of sitting on their arses all day talking about aigs?

As I got closer to work I worried less about Frank and Ralph's wives and more about Mr. Chen. I wondered if he'd still be mad about earlier.

I tapped lightly on the back door.

Tum-ti-ti-tum-tum.

The door swung open.

Tum-tum!

I was pretty sure getting bonked twice in the head with a chicken-wing sign was against some kind of workplace health and safety rules, but the grin on Mr. Chen's face suggested it was all fun and games.

I rubbed my head. "I guess we're even now?"

He passed me my sign. "Get to work, Poppy Flower."

Just as he turned his attention back to the deep-fat fryer, two new customers arrived and the telephone started ringing.

"You know, you should get some extra help," I said. "This job will be the death of you."

He waved me away. "You worry about your job, Nosy Parker, and I'll worry about mine."

I marched up and down Elgin hoping I'd see Miracle again. Halfway through my shift she showed up.

"I told my friends about you," she said. "Buck wants to meet you so that he can ask why you cross the road."

I laughed out loud.

"I told you he was funny."

She was wearing a T-shirt with a cartoon narwhal on the front. It said, *Always be yourself. Unless you can be a narwhal. Then always be a narwhal.*

As she walked alongside me I asked, "Miracle? What do you want to be when you grow up?"

I was hoping for astronaut or prime minister. I got backup dancer.

"Watch this," she said.

She did a backwards flip on the spot.

"Whoa," I said. "How did you do that?"

She shrugged. "Practice."

I stood firmly on my giant chicken feet and imagined flipping backwards. I rocked my hips back and forth and pumped my arms. All I produced was a pathetic little hop. Miracle laughed.

"How do you get the guts?" I said. "To just throw yourself backwards like that?"

"You have to be brave," she said.

"Well, I'm a chicken," I said. "So that's not going to happen."

We continued our walk. I could feel droplets of sweat rolling from the small of my back to the inside of my underwear. I wondered if there was such a thing as butt-crack deodorant.

Miracle skipped beside me. "Will you come under the bridge tonight?" she asked.

I shrugged. "Maybe."

"Don't come as a chicken, okay? I want you as you."

I don't think she knew how beautiful that was.

When we got to Chen Chicken she hugged me. "I have to go home now. Lewis will be taking me under the bridge soon."

I wanted to know why but thought it best not to ask.

Mr. Chen popped his head out of the shop. "Merry-girl. Come here!"

"Wait," I said. "You know her?"

He passed her a family pack of chicken wings and fries. "Bring this home. Share with your mother. And don't ever put a rubber chicken in my deep-fat fryer again."

I turned to Miracle. "You put a rubber chicken in the deep-fat fryer?"

Miracle hugged him around the waist. "Thank you, Mr. Chen."

When she disappeared down Elgin Street I said, "How do you know her?"

He looked me up and down. "You always did strike me as a busybody."

"Always?" I said. "Pfssh! I've only known you three weeks."

He scratched his head. "Really? Feels like an eternity."
He went into the shop and shut the door behind him.
Busybody or not, I wanted to know Miracle's story.
And there was only one way to find out.

CHAPTER TWO

Cam was in his room getting dressed for a party. I was in mine watching hidden-camera video of a baby being slapped by its babysitter. It was my new normal, the sick feeling in the pit of my stomach.

Cam begged me to go with him, to the end-of-year bash in the suburbs. But I didn't want to have fun in a house with no walls. I wanted to stay within the confines of my own and be miserable.

Mom knocked on my door. "Your father and I are going to a movie. Want to come?"

Lying came easy now. "I'm going to a party with Cam."

"You are?" she said. "That's nice."

I stood up, looked in my closet. She looked beyond me, her eyes falling onto my collection of vintage clothes. "You should wear something fun," she said. "Like you used to."

It didn't feel right dressing up, not when babies were being slapped by their babysitters.

I threw a decoy outfit on the bed.

Mom smiled. "Have fun tonight, okay?"

When the door clicked shut I sat back on my bed.

Like you used to. She'd been noticing. She'd be asking questions soon—what was wrong, was everything okay. Cam promised not to tell—she'd only worry. He kept his word. Even when I was at risk of internal organ damage.

I clipped my high-waisted navy sailor shorts with white button accents onto a pants hanger and neatly folded my red-and-white-striped crop top onto a shelf.

Then I got in bed and cried until I was a bag of skin filled with organs and bones.

⚜

It was Christmas Day when I stumbled across the Fans of the Forties forum. I thought I'd found my people. I loved scrolling through the photos of community members in their thrift-store finds, so much so that I decided to post a photo of myself—as Rosie the Riveter. Cam was immediately on board. We spent hours in our little living room, setting up the backdrop with a bright-yellow bedsheet from the Salvation Army store and using various lamps to get the lighting just right. Cam did my makeup and helped pick the outfit. In the spirit of mixing vintage and modern styles I wore a denim shirt tied at the midriff, a pair of skinny jeans, and red Converse sneaker boots. The pose, of course, remained the same. Cam and I loved the result. So did my people on the forum. The comments filled with words like *fun, fresh, stunning.* They even complimented my body, but not in a way that felt objectifying. They said things like *Now there's a girl who owns her curves. Amazing!* and *Finally, a Rosie re-creation portraying a classic, healthy body type. Bravo!*

I was riding the wave of a social-media high.

A week later, I was drowning.

The message came from a user of the forum: *Sorry. Thought you should know.* They included a link to a subreddit.

It was called ISeeFatPeople.

My stomach tightened as the page loaded.

There I was. Me, as Rosie the Riveter. Except now, instead of holding a kick-ass fist in the air, I was holding a hamburger. *My* photo became *The* Photo. It had a life of its own. It had nothing to do with me and everything to do with me.

I wondered who did it. One of "my people" from the forum? A random person who spends all day trolling various websites for people who are not their ideal body weight?

I was so confused.

It was interesting how the addition of the burger had changed the language used to describe my body from *healthy* and *amazing* to *gross* and *disgusting.*

Their comments weren't even that clever.

Rosie the Riveter? More like Rosie the Picnicker.

Somebody *ate all the rations.*

They called me Hambeast, Monster, Landwhale, Butterbeast.

Being a target hurt.

But what hurt more was that I'd tarnished the image of Rosie the Riveter with my supposedly gross and disgusting body.

~~~~

When my room darkened I got out of bed. I pulled a brush through my hair and thought about Miracle. I wondered if she had a computer. I hoped she didn't.

I pinned my hair back and looked at the bandana that hung on the corner of my mirror.

I remembered Miracle's words. *I want you as you.*

I brought the bandana to my nose, breathed the Rosieness in.

I may have been jaded, but Miracle didn't have to be.

I took a breath and tied the bandana around my head, Rosie style, with the ends tied into a knot on top.

Maybe Miracle would ask me about it and I could tell her about the badass girls of the forties.

I went to Cam's room and borrowed his Chanel Rouge Allure lipstick. My hand shook as I applied it. For a moment

I wished I was getting ready for roller derby. I wanted to pull a pair of short shorts over some fishnets and top it off with a Rosie-inspired polka-dotted crop top. I wanted to pump myself up by watching videos of the Brawlipops' previous jams, then go to the arena and skate my ass off. But I'd just be pretending. It was best to keep it real—and I had a feeling that under the bridge was as real as it got.

As I walked through the downtown core I sent Cam a text: *I'm not home I'm with you.* He knew exactly what I meant.

Cam always had my back.

I stood on the Fifth Street bridge wondering what Miracle was doing below. I wondered again why she went there, at nine o'clock at night when she should have been sleeping in bed.

The embankment was steep so I walked on an angle to keep my footing. Miracle jumped up when she saw me. "You came as you!"

Stupidly, crazily, weirdly, my eyes filled with tears. I blinked them away. She put her arms up to be lifted. I wasn't used to kids. She was heavier than she looked. She wrapped her legs around my waist. Her hair smelled like Johnson's baby shampoo. A moment later, she was wriggling out of my grasp. "Come meet my friends."

They were sitting on a concrete platform at the base of the bridge.

"This is Lewis," she said, plunking into his lap. "My very best pal."

I liked his hair. It was stubbly on the back and sides, like Miracle had said, but on the top was a slicked-back quiff, jet black with a hint of red dye. He had great bone structure.

She introduced Thumper next. He wasn't quite one hundred years old but his beard and hair were as white as snow. He looked like Santa, if Santa were skinny with a ponytail and a motorcycle tattoo.

Miracle whispered, "Thumper has arse-ritis."

I whispered back, "Maybe he should take some ass-pirin."

The third guy, who I assumed was Buck, said, "Come on over, Chicken Girl."

He was English. Cam would die. He loved a British accent.

I sat beside him. "Because the light was green."

He laughed. The others looked confused.

"It's why she crossed the road," said Buck.

"Wow," said Lewis. "A private joke. And they've only known each other two minutes."

Buck moved close to me. His arm was an inch away from mine. I felt a tingling, from the top of my shoulder to the tips of my fingers. I had that surreal chicken feeling. Something was happening but I wasn't sure what.

Even though it was summer, Lewis built a fire on the concrete platform and put a blanket around Thumper's shoulders. A spark landed near my foot. It made a loud pop, like the crack of a spine on a new book.

Maybe that's what this was—a new chapter.

Buck looked at my lips. "That color is brilliant."

It was a kick-ass opening line.

I gave him a quick once-over. His white T-shirt and jeans looked as if they'd just been pressed, and his suede desert boots were spotless. His permanently flushed cheeks gave him a wholesome, outdoorsy look, like he'd walked straight out of a print ad for high-end outerwear. I was so taken with his appearance I said, "You don't look like you live under a bridge."

He laughed. "I wasn't aware homelessness had a particular look."

"It's just that you look really nice," I said. "You smell nice too."

"What about the rest of us?" said Lewis. "Do we look homeless?"

He looked nice too—in an edgier way. I liked the way he cuffed his jeans over his red Converse. I was about to tell him that when Miracle brought her T-shirt to her nose. "Do I smell? I hope I don't smell."

I wanted to back up—to the prologue. I wanted to be standing on the bridge wondering about Miracle below.

"Just so you know," said Lewis, "only half of us are homeless."

I wondered which half.

"And some of us," said Thumper, "are homeless by choice."

I was confused. "Why would anyone be homeless by choice?"

Miracle looked confused too. "Why do you look like that, Poppy?"

"Like what?"

"Like there's a stink under your nose."

Thumper smiled. His eyes were as blue as Cam's Sea the Point nail polish. He said, "Some people like to live in the outdoors because they don't like to be tied down."

I said, "But being tied down keeps you from drifting away."

The others looked at me as if it was an odd thing to say, but Thumper said, "You say that like it's a bad thing."

Miracle sat back in Lewis's lap. She held Gilbert in her fist and sucked her thumb. The fingers of her other hand stroked the shaved bits on the side of Lewis's head.

We listened to Thumper's stories. He told us about his travels, how he'd lived in yurts and houseboats and caravans. He said no matter how far he traveled, or where he was, he called each place home. He said he connected with each and every person he met, no matter how wild and crazy they were. He said their songs and stories were like medicine and he gulped them down, every last drop. *Because that's what it's all about,* he said. *Connections.*

Maybe, I thought, Thumper could be a portal, out of the darkness and into something new. I'd jump in with two feet and I'd never look back. I could see the world through his skinny Santa eyes and close the chicken ones forever.

At eleven o'clock, everyone moved from the center of the platform to their spots along the perimeter. Lewis settled Thumper under a blanket, then moved farther along and settled Miracle into a hot-pink sleeping bag. He lay down beside her.

I moved with Buck to his spot near the embankment.

He nudged me with his elbow. "Want some?"

I looked down. There was a joint on his palm.

Chapter one had come to an end and a new one was just beginning.

I glanced over at the others. "It's just a bit of weed," said Buck. "It'll take you away from whatever you're running from."

I frowned. "I'm not running from anything." At least I didn't think I was.

He lit the joint and passed it to me.

I wanted to see how chapter two played out so I took it.

I tried to look cool holding it. He said, "First time?"

I nodded.

"It's okay, darlin'. We can take it slow."

He put it between his lips and took a long, deep inhale, then he put it between mine. I didn't even cough.

"You're a good student," he said.

"You're a good teacher."

When the joint was gone he stood up. "I need a wee. Back in a tick."

I looked around. Thumper waved me over.

"Watch yourself with Prince Charming," he whispered. "Before you know it, you'll have no brain cells."

I shrugged. "It's just a bit of weed."

I nodded at the book that lay in his lap. "You read the Bible?"

He smiled. "I *wrote* the bible."

He opened it up. Handwritten pages were taped over the originals.

I laughed. "You might go to hell for that."

"I'm not worried," he said. "Jesus loves the hell out of everyone."

I reached down and flipped through the pages. "You rewrote the whole thing?"

He grinned. "The old one was too open to interpretation." Then he tucked his bible into a leather satchel. "Go on," he said. "Back to your prince. He'll be back in a minute."

When Buck returned he settled in close. "Hungry?"

He reached into his messenger bag and passed me a banana. I started to peel it the normal way, from the stem, but he took it back.

"Do it the monkey way."

He turned it upside-down, peeled it from the nubby end.

"Now you've got a handle," he said, holding the stem.

I smiled. "Say *banana*."

"Why?"

"Just say it."

"Ba-naw-naw."

Adorable.

"Are you taking the mick?"

"I like the way you talk, that's all."

People say Brits have bad teeth. His were perfect.

After we ate, he slipped into his sleeping bag. He opened the flap for me to join him.

I wanted things to feel surreal again so I could blame what I was about to do on a dreamlike state. But suddenly, things felt very real.

I kicked off my shoes and got in beside him.

The ground felt hard beneath my head. He put out his arm. I laid my head on it.

"I have a headache," I whispered.

He kissed my forehead. I could feel his warmth. I was sleepy and tingly all at the same time.

"I'm sorry for saying that you smelled nice," I said, "as if being homeless meant that you shouldn't. It was very hobophobic of me."

He laughed. "I prefer the term *tramp*, thank you very much."

"Does that make me Lady?" I said. "You know, from that Disney movie?"

"Yes," he said. "You are a beautiful cocker spaniel and I am a mutt."

He put his hand on my hip. I hated myself for sucking in. I thought I was over that.

I said, "Did you know that Peggy Lee was the voice of Lady's owner?"

He inched closer. "Who's Peggy Lee?"

I sucked in more.

"A singer."

The lyrics to "I'm a Woman" ran through my head. Peggy could clean the house, feed the baby, fix the car, go swingin' till four, sleep at five, wake at six, and do it all over again. There was nothing she couldn't do because she was a W-O-M-A-N.

And here I was, putting my internal organs at risk because of some guy.

I breathed out. "We should do the spaghetti thing sometime."

"That ends with a kiss, you know."

"Yeah," I said. "I know."

I cuddled into him. "You know, I always wondered why the Tramp called Lady 'Pidge.'"

"It's a term of endearment," he said. "Short for *pigeon.*"

He closed his eyes. I was tempted to stay the night but I had my one o'clock curfew to think of.

I closed my eyes, just for a minute.

I was woken by a rustling. "What's going on?"

"Lewis is taking Miracle home," said Buck. "Her mother's tricks will be gone by now."

Tricks?

Miracle's mother sells herself. I was sinking through concrete, every part of me. I wrapped my arms around Buck's waist.

"You okay, love?"

All was quiet, except for the trickling of the river. I looked at the time on my phone. It was 12:45. I was going to be late. "I should go home now."

He offered me his cheek. I kissed him on the lips.

He smiled. "Goodbye, Pidge."

Except for a few passing cars, the streets were quiet. I walked through the downtown core, then followed the tracks back toward home. I was surprised to see Lewis coming out of one of the pathways that led to my neighborhood. He looked surprised to see me, too.

"Buck didn't walk with you?"

"Why would he?" I said. "It wasn't far."

He looked unimpressed. "Still."

I sighed. "Being female doesn't make me a delicate little flower, you know."

He smiled. "I think it's safer to walk in pairs, that's all."

We walked side by side up the path.

"I didn't know Miracle lived around here."

He nodded. "She's over on Victoria."

"Oooh!" I said. "She lives in a Victory house too!"

I proceeded to give him a history lesson on Canadian wartime houses. I said, "Victory homes were built to house factory workers and soldiers returning from war. They were supposed to be temporary, but the neighborhoods became so strong they lasted long after the war." I wrapped up with "Pretty cool, huh?" to which he replied, "He's older than you, you know."

I knew who he was talking about and wondered why he cared. "So?"

"He's twenty."

I shrugged. "As my mother says, age is not important unless you're a cheese."

He snorted. "Yeah, well, Buck's a big hunk of old British cheddar."

I laughed. "You don't like him, do you?"

"I barely know him. He showed up a few months ago, said he was just passing through."

"Well, I happen to like British cheddar," I said. "It's got a real zing."

"I prefer Canadian," said Lewis. "It's smoother and more well-rounded. You should give it a try sometime."

I stole a sideways glance at him. He had broad shoulders and a muscly chest. On his left arm was a black armband tattoo. He caught me looking at it.

"In memory of my mom. She died when I was five."

"I'm sorry."

"This, on the other hand," he said, "is just for fun."

A miniature Pinocchio stood proudly on the inside of his wrist.

"'Now, remember, Pinocchio,'" I said, quoting the Blue Fairy. "'Be a good boy and always let your conscience be your guide.'"

Lewis smiled. "Always."

At the bottom of Churchill I said, "Well, thanks for walking me—I mean, thanks for *accompanying* me."

He smiled. "No problem."

Cam was in the driveway, hiding in the shadows. "We're twenty minutes late."

"The house is dark," I said. "They'll never know."

We climbed the stairs together. On the landing he said, "Oh, Poppy. I just noticed."

"Noticed what?"

He reached up, touched my bandana.

I didn't mean to get his hopes up.

"I only wore it so I could tell a little girl about Rosie the Riveter."

"The little girl in the polka-dot socks?"

I nodded.

"And did you?"

I shook my head. "She never asked."

He looked at me with curiosity. "Where were you tonight, Pops?"

I slid the bandana off my head. "I was in another world."

He frowned. "Are you high?"

"Pfssh. No."

I went to bed. A few minutes later Cam crept in. I didn't have to ask what he wanted. He was going to create a cross-breeze—he always did on particularly sticky nights. He'd open his window, then mine, and leave the doors open in between.

He crossed the room to the small sash window I always had difficulty opening. It was easy for him. He was as lean as Buck but as strong as Lewis. Another reason I wished he'd get back into boxing. It's like they say, use it or lose it. I didn't want Cam to lose it. I wanted him to be strong forever.

When Cam left the room I closed my eyes and pictured the words *Chapter One*. I wanted to relive my night under the bridge but the page was out of focus. As I drifted off, a warm summer breeze floated in through my window, lifting the letters off the page.

In the morning Cam was sitting at his vanity, plucking his eyebrows.

I sat on his bed and talked to his reflection. "So. How was your night with the Drome-drearies?"

"Awesome. Now enough about me. Spill."

I rolled my eyes. "You'd swear I'd never had a night out before."

"You haven't," he said. "Well, not in the last six months anyway."

"By the way," I said, "I borrowed your lipstick. The Chanel Allure."

He paused his plucking and looked me in the eye. "What's with the procrastination, Pops? Did you rob a bank or something?"

"Pfssh. No."

"So where were you last night?"

"I was just, you know, hanging out . . . under the Fifth Street bridge."

"Ew, Pops. Why?"

"The little girl with the polka-dot socks, she invited me. There's this one guy, Buck, and—"

"Buck? Sounds like a hillbilly."

"Pfssh. Far from it. He's . . . British."

Cam's eyes lit up.

"Really? England, Ireland, Scotland, or Wales?"

"England."

"Oooh. Does he say, *All right, guv'nor? 'Ow's yer fatha?*"

"He's not the chimney sweep from *Mary Poppins*."

"Does he say *gobsmacked*? Love that word."

"No. But he says *brilliant* like *brill-e-ant* and when he called me darling he said it without the *g*."

Cam tried it out.

"'Allo, darlin'. 'Ow 'bout we go for a pint o' lager down at the ol' Bangers and Mash."

I laughed. "What the hell, Cam?"

"The pubs over there always have names like that," he said. "The Fox and the Hound. The Lady and the Tramp."

"Oooh," I said. "The Lady and the Tramp—that's kind of our thing."

"Thing?" he said. "How can you have a thing? You've only known him five minutes."

I grinned. "He kissed me."

It was the other way round but Cam didn't need to know that.

"You should see his hair," I said. "It's this big wavy mop that's streaked with a bunch of shades of blond. He runs his fingers through it to keep it out of his face and it goes all swoopy on the top."

Cam swooned. "Sounds amazing. Would he happen to have a gay twin brother?"

I kept going. "He looks like one of those models from that clothing brand that you like."

"Burberry? Jesus, Poppy. Why don't you just stab me to death with my tweezers? Here, take them. Kill me now."

I laughed. "I think I really like him."

Cam stood up. "I'm happy for you, Pops."

He pulled on a dress shirt and grinned. "And you can be happy for me when I get this job."

I smiled. "You have an interview?"

"Yup," he said. "At Bliss."

"The hair salon?"

I must have looked like there was a stink under my nose because Cam sighed and said, "What's the problem, Pops?"

I shrugged. "I thought you didn't want a summer job."

"I didn't," he said, "but then I met the owner of Bliss at Starbucks. He came over to my table to tell me I had great hair. He is *so* nice. He said he was looking for an assistant—you know, someone to sweep hair and stuff."

I snorted. "You? Sweep hair?"

"If you must know," he said, "it's an entry-level position. Eventually, I can move up."

"To what?" I said. "You want to be a hairdresser now?"

He pulled a tie out of his closet. "You know, Poppy. Sometimes I don't feel totally supported by you."

"Don't say that, Cam."

I stood up, helped him with his collar. "All I want is for you to be happy."

He looked me in the eye. "I *am* happy."

I forced a smile. "Good."

I watched him tie the tie the way Dad taught him, with the fox chasing the rabbit, around the tree and down the hole.

He put on some bronzer and fixed his hair.

My sweet Cam. I was glad he thought he was happy.

But I couldn't help but wonder if he'd be happier working at the boxing club.

Maybe I'll mention it later, I thought. *When he's not so touchy.*

I went to my room and watched a montage of swing dancers during the big-band era. I pictured myself doing the Lindy Hop with Buck.

I wondered why he was homeless. It seemed rude to ask.

I googled homelessness in the forties. Between 1939 and 1945 people were able to escape the streets by going to war. It really was the best of times.

I pictured Buck in uniform signing up for active duty. Thumper would be too old. Then again, he liked living rough. That, I'd never understand.

I was about to google prostitution in the forties but then I remembered it was the world's oldest profession. I wondered why Miracle's mother didn't just get a job at McDonald's or Tim Hortons. Or apply for the lunchtime gig at Chen Chicken. Surely anything was better than selling your body for money.

I visited ISeeFatPeople. Someone had posted a photo of an overweight person on a train with the caption *Ham on a train, taking up all my leg space.*

I wondered where the "ham" was going. Maybe they were going to work. Or the movies.

Their obliviousness made my heart ache.

I thought about Buck. Even if we fell in love and had a wild summer romance, there'd still be injustice in the world.

Maybe I should just let him take me away from it all. It's like he said, it's only a bit of weed.

CHAPTER THREE

I ate a handful of Honeycombs for breakfast and headed
down to the bridge. Thumper's brow was furrowed but he
smiled when he saw me. I sat beside him. "Your arse-ritis?"

He laughed. "Yes. And I'm fresh out of ass-pirin."

I looked around. "Where is everyone?"

"Lewis leaves first thing," he said. "And Buck is gone to
get Miracle. She likes to have breakfast with us."

He rubbed his joints to ease the pain. They were fat
and swollen—not only the knuckles but the smaller joints
near his fingertips.

"I'm sorry if I seemed judgmental last night," I said. "I
didn't think people would want to be homeless by choice."

"Don't worry, Poppy. We're all different. It'd be a boring
world if we weren't."

He switched from rubbing his left hand with his right
to rubbing his right hand with his left. One knobbly hand
trying to soothe the other. It was as fruitless as putting out
fire with fire.

"Different is overrated," I said. "If people were all the same, with the same values and beliefs, they wouldn't hurt each other. There probably wouldn't even be wars."

His face filled with concern.

"The world is good, Poppy. It's not perfect, but it's good."

His leather satchel was between us on his blanket. I ran my fingers across it. "Thumper? Is it okay to be gay in your bible?"

"Of course it is," he said.

It was weird how relieved I felt.

"Sometimes I watch things I shouldn't," I said. "I saw a video once of a gay kid being lured to an apartment, only to be beaten."

His concern turned to sadness. "You shouldn't watch things like that."

"I know," I said. "But if I hadn't seen it, I wouldn't know, and if I didn't know, I'd be living in a bubble."

"I lived in a bubble once," he said. "With a bunch of hippies down in Arizona."

I laughed. "Sounds great. But the problem with bubbles is, they tend to pop."

"Not this one," he said. "It was made of a very durable plastic."

He grinned at me and I grinned back.

I reached over and took his hand. "Let me try."

I worked my way up each finger, gently rubbing each joint.

"How long have you been living down here?" I asked.

"Eight months," he said. "There were twenty of us here once."

"I saw this documentary," I said, "about a homeless camp under an expressway. People stole each other's stuff and one of the women got sexually assaulted."

He shook his head. "I think you need to change your viewing habits. Why don't you try, I don't know, *Looney Tunes?*"

I did my best Porky Pig impression. "'Th-th-th-tha-tha-tha-that's all, folks!'"

When Thumper laughed his eyes twinkled like the ocean. I switched to his other hand.

He nodded to a margarine container. "By the way," he said, "that's our snub tub . . . if you find yourself needing to say sorry again."

Knowing me, I probably would.

"How much do people usually put in?" I asked.

"We don't add money," he said. "We add words, things we should have said instead."

I picked up the tub. "Do you think I can add something now?"

"Of course," he said. "You'll find a pencil and paper inside."

I opened the lid. The tub was filled with slips of paper. There was one on the top that read:

Lewis,
You actually don't look like you've had a fight with a lawn mower. Your new haircut is smashing.
Cheers,
Buck

"I've met a lot of people in my travels," said Thumper, "and not everyone sees eye to eye. That tub has solved many a problem and made forever friends out of potential enemies."

I wrote my message with a tiny pencil and slipped it into the bottom of the tub.

I put the lid on and looked around.

"It *is* nice down here," I said. "Even if there are no walls."

"It's nice down here," he said, "*because* there are no walls."

I was about to tell him about the house in the suburbs when Buck and Miracle rounded the corner.

"Mama made breakfast," said Miracle.

Buck looked surprised, and happy, to see me. "Good morning, Pidge."

I moved with Buck to his sleeping area, where we ate warm blueberry muffins.

When we were done he said, "Want a tour of the city?"

"Not particularly," I said. "I've lived here all my life."

He pulled a camera out of the messenger bag he never seemed to be without. "You haven't seen it the way I do."

Powerful images appeared on his display screen. One in particular was striking. He'd caught a woman smoking a cigarette mid-puff. Her cheeks were sucked inward. Her eyes were wide but thoughtful.

"How do you do that?" I asked.

"Do what?"

"Make stuff beautiful."

He said it like it was obvious. "*Truth* is beautiful."

He left out the *t*. *Beau'iful.*

He clicked to the next image. A girl of about six, a face full of joy, as if what she was kicking down the alley was a soccer ball, not a beer can. I could almost hear the rattle of metal against pavement.

He continued scrolling. The photos were breathtaking and stark. Some were haunting.

Buck looked from his camera to me. "You've gone quiet."

I wanted to share my pain with him.

"I was in a photo once."

Wrinkles formed across his forehead. "What kind of photo?"

I took out my phone, showed him the original.

"Bloody hell," he said. "You look as fit as a butcher's dog."

I laughed. "Is that good?"

He raised his eyebrows. "Very."

I shoved the phone back in my pocket. "I thought I looked good too."

"You don't anymore?"

Suddenly, I didn't feel like talking.

Buck put his hand under my chin, directed my face toward his. "Come on, love. You can tell me."

It hurt to think of, let alone say out loud.

"Someone posted it on a subreddit," I said. "But they . . ."

He took my hand. "They what?"

"They photoshopped a hamburger in my fist."

A smile spread slowly across his lips.

"It's not funny," I said.

He smirked. "It kind of is."

I stood up. "Goodbye, Buck."

He hopped to his feet. "Come on, Poppy. What's the big deal?"

"You don't get it, do you?" I said. "I was being mocked. Because I'm not as skinny as a rail."

He put his hands on my hips. "And thank God for that."

I pushed him away. "Get your hands off me."

Thumper cleared his throat from across the platform. "You okay, Poppy?"

I nodded. "I was just leaving."

Buck reached for my arm. "Don't be like that, Poppy. I'm just saying. Being chunky is what makes you so hot."

I pulled away. "Really?" I said. "*Chunky*? Is that supposed to be a compliment?"

He shrugged. "Why not? I mean, who doesn't like a good chocolate chunk cookie? And chunky peanut butter is way better than smooth."

"Word of advice," I said. "Comparing me to fattening foods is not helping."

"Come on, Pidge. You should embrace your body. It's gorgeous."

"I *do* embrace my body," I said. "I'm a brick shithouse, for God's sake. You should see me playing roller derby."

He took a step back. "Wait now. What? You skate around in skimpy clothing, manhandling other women? When do you play? Can I come watch?"

I ignored him.

"The thing is," I said, "my body is not the problem. The problem is that random people think they have the right to stick hamburgers in my hand and post it on the internet!"

"Oh, please," he said. "It was one hamburger and it was a joke."

I looked at him like he was dense, which he was. "Why am I still talking to you?" I said. "Obviously you don't get it. And you never will."

I turned away and stormed up the embankment.

"You know, Pidge," he called, "sometimes in life you've just got to laugh at yourself."

I called back, loud enough for the whole world to hear. "Well, ha freakin' ha."

When I got home I went straight to the fridge. I took out a yogurt, a cheese string, a piece of salami, and an apple. If there was a fly on the wall, that fly might have thought I was comfort eating, but actually I was just hungry.

There's a general assumption that if you're a bit on the heavier side you have food issues. Not me. My relationship with food was pretty healthy.

Except for that one time at Swiss Chalet. Cam asked if he could have the rest of my Chalet sauce and I handed it over, like a crazy person. The rest of my fries too. It was because The Photo had been posted the day before and I was hearing the echoes. It was as if someone with a great, booming voice had yelled the comments into a cave—a twisted, sinister cave that holds echoes in its belly, releasing them when you least expect it.

Later, at home, Cam lectured me in my bedroom. He paced back and forth in a black bodysuit and heels (he'd been dancing to Beyoncé in his room). He said I was letting them win, that he hadn't actually expected me to hand over my Chalet sauce—it was the nectar of the gods, for Christ's sake. He said, "What the hell, Pops, you're going to start dieting now?"

"God, no," I said.

He stopped strutting long enough to wave a pointed finger at my face. "Never, ever, give up your Chalet sauce again. Got it?"

I nodded. "You'd have to pry it out of my cold, dead hands."

"And don't think I didn't see you looking sideways in the mirror this morning with your gut sucked in," he said.

"I was just wondering what I'd look like if I was thin," I said.

"Well, get over it," he said. "You weren't meant to be thin. Just like I wasn't meant to be straight."

"I had a lapse in judgment," I said. "I'm fine, really. I'm happy with who I am."

He stuck out his pinkie. "Promise?"

I wrapped mine tightly around his. "Promise."

It was true. I loved who I was. But the echoes were like hiccups. You never knew when you were going to get them. Maybe I would, in a moment of weakness, suck in my gut again. I hoped not but you never could tell.

I finished my snack and cleaned away the garbage. On my way upstairs I grabbed a handful of cereal. I hoped the echoes would never stop me from eating Honeycombs. I liked them way too much.

———✒———

I spent the afternoon watching videos that Thumper would disapprove of. The first one was called "Bum Bashing: Part One." In it, a gang of teenagers set a homeless man on fire. I couldn't find Part Two but I hoped he'd been put out.

I had to stop doing this.

I got up and looked out my window. Frank was watering his lawn. Ralph was leaning on the fence. They were probably talking about "aigs" or the price of gas or what their wives were making for supper. It must be nice to have nothing to think about.

I sat back on my bed and wondered what it felt like to be burned alive.

I forced myself to watch happy things. I started with a clip of the Andrews Sisters singing "Don't Sit under the Apple Tree (With Anyone Else but Me)." A song about sweethearts separated by war really lifted my spirits.

Then I watched "Boogie Woogie Bugle Boy." I played the air bugle, complete with sound effects.

I didn't watch roller derby. It'd only make me sad. It

was the same as hanging out with Eve. Being with the best would make things the worst. Why highlight the things I no longer had, even if it was by choice?

A sparrow landed on my windowsill. I wondered how old it was. It was hard to tell. When it flew away I googled "lifespan of a sparrow." Three years. A few clicks later I was reading about the plight of endangered animals. We humans are terrible people.

I went to Cam's room.

"Say something funny."

He looked up from his magazine. "Don't you hate it when people answer their own questions? I do."

I smiled. "Good one."

His dress shirt and tie were draped across the bottom of his bed.

"So," I said. "Did you get it?"

He nodded. "I start tomorrow."

I tried to sound enthusiastic. "Awesome."

He wasn't buying it.

I said, "You know, they might have a summer job at the boxing club."

He snapped his magazine open and started reading again. "They might have had a summer job at the roller rink too."

I smiled. "Touché."

He didn't smile back.

I walked over to him, bent down to hug him. "I love you, Cam."

He smiled. "Don't worry, Pops. I know you do."

I put on my chicken costume. It smelled like the inside of an old gym sock. Especially the head. I googled "stinky mascot costume" and clicked on the first result—*Amazing Mascot Cleaning Trick—WOW!* I decided to give it a try. I filled an old Lysol bottle with half water and half whiskey (it was supposed to be vodka but the pickings were slim in my parents' liquor cabinet, and I figured alcohol was alcohol). I liberally sprayed the inside of the chicken head and let it sit for a few minutes, then wiped out the excess with a cloth. The fumes made my eyes water and I wondered if alcohol *wasn't* alcohol and vodka was meant to be used because it has a less offensive smell than whiskey. I googled "how to reduce strong whiskey smells" but the results were about getting the stench off your breath, not the inside of your head, so I walked to work stinking like an intoxicated chicken.

Miracle was on the steps of Chen Chicken, pouting.

I sat beside her and took my head off. "What's up?"

She sniffed the air. "You smell like Mama's friends."

"I washed my head with a special cleaner," I said, hoping that would satisfy her. It did.

"Mr. Chen is mad at me."

"Why?"

"He said I was ripping people off, but I was trying to help them."

"Help who?" I asked.

"The poor people on James Street."

"You were on James Street?"

"This morning. I told them if they rubbed it every day they'd have good luck."

"Rubbed what?"

"The chicken feet I took from the kitchen. I sold them for a dollar a piece!"

"Miracle!"

"Mama's friend wears one around his neck. He said it brings him good juju."

Mr. Chen appeared behind us. I stood up and pulled him aside.

"I'll take her to James Street," I whispered. "After my shift. We'll return the money."

He sniffed the air. "What's that smell?"

I sniffed the air too. "What smell?"

He sighed. "Just take her now," he said. "I'm too tired to deal with this."

I followed his gaze. "Why would she do such a thing?"

"She's a monkey," he said. "That's why."

I sat back down beside her.

"If you want to talk about me behind my back," she said, "you should speak Mandarin. That's what Lewis does when he talks about me to Mr. Chen."

I laughed. "Do I look like I know Mandarin?"

She looked me up and down. "Anything's possible with practice," she said. "That's what Mama says."

I glanced back at Mr. Chen. "I didn't know you knew Lewis."

"His father is a good friend," said Mr. Chen.

"He might die soon," said Miracle. "Mama said that too."

Mr. Chen cleared his throat. "I should get back to the kitchen."

Miracle looked at her shoes. "Lewis's birthday is soon. Everyone's chipping in. I wanted to chip in too."

Mr. Chen paused. "If you wanted money, Merry-girl, all you had to do was ask."

I picked up my head and followed him into the shop.

"Are you okay, Mr. Chen? You look like hell."

He twitched his nose like a hound on the scent of a rabbit.

"Have you been drinking, Poppy Flower?"

I glanced down at the head tucked under my arm. "No."

He looked at me suspiciously and held out his hands. "Can I see that a minute?"

He brought the head toward his face.

"I wouldn't do that if I were you."

He took a big whiff.

"Holy moly!"

His eyes watered like Niagara Falls.

"The internet said vodka would do the trick," I said. "But I only had whiskey."

He was fuming, like the head. "What trick?"

"The cleaning trick," I said.

He sniffed the head again, lightly this time. "Did you wear this on the way here?"

I nodded. Anonymity was a must, no matter how bad the conditions.

He shook his head. "It's a wonder you're not as drunk as a skunk."

I tried to lighten the mood.

"That's a bit prejudiced, don't you think?" I said. "Not *all* skunks are alcoholics. Just the ones that live on James Street."

Mr. Chen shot me a look and said something about people in glass houses. He was making no sense. It must have been the fumes.

I took off my chicken suit and hung it next to the empty hook that rarely held Mr. Chen's apron.

"Well," I said, "I should go."

I was looking forward to a couple of hours off. Even if it did mean going to James Street to right the wrong of a six-year-old girl selling chicken feet.

The feel of her little hands in mine ...

The way she looked up every now and then and smiled ...

The flashing lights of the rubber soles of her Mary Jane shoes.

I wanted a ray gun—one that could not only freeze time but loop it. I'd live my life on a thirty-second repeat— me and Miracle walking down James Street, her looking up at me, me looking down at her—clip-clop, flash, flash, repeat. The loop would begin just after we stepped over a pile of vomit and end just as I hid her eyes from a flasher. We'd never need know that happiness was temporary.

James Street was full of characters that Miracle was way too friendly with.

"That's where Dodgy Dick lives," she said, pointing to a window above a tattoo parlor. "He put baby powder in cocaine and the people who bought it from him got mad and beat him up."

I was pretty sure the only coke consumed in the forties came in a bottle with a red-and-white label. I pictured Miracle in a soda shop wearing saddle shoes and bobby socks and wished that time machines were real.

"And that's where MaJonna lives," she said. She pointed to a window above Massage and More.

I dreaded to think what the More was.

"He's a Madonna impersonal-ater," she said. "He went on tour but then he got hit by a car and now he doesn't think right. He wears bare feet, even on the pavement, but when he's Madonna he wears heels."

I sighed and nodded toward the baggie of loose change in her hand. "Can we just get this done?"

Miracle tried to give out refunds, but most people were happy with the promise of good juju and declined the offer.

She jingled her coins. "Do I have to give this money to Mr. Chen? Because they were his chicken feet? Or can I keep it?"

"I think Mr. Chen would want you to have it."

"Even though he's mad at me?"

"He won't be mad anymore. Not now that you've righted a wrong."

She looked up at me. "I righted a wrong?"

"You sure did."

She looked at her baggie. "Do you think it would be okay if I saved half of these coins for Lewis's birthday and gave the other half to the next homeless person I see?"

I tweaked her nose. "I think that would be more than okay."

She put half the coins in her pocket, then took my hand. I wished she had a hand to hold all day long.

"Miracle?"

"Yes?"

"You probably shouldn't hang out down here on your own."

"Why not?"

"Because you're only little."

"Little? I told you, I'm six!"

"Still, maybe you should stick to Elgin Street."

As we crossed James and York she said, "Look! It's Buck!"

He was taking pictures of a homeless man and the man's dog in the doorway of an abandoned building.

Miracle tugged on my arm. "Come on."

Up ahead, Buck and the man traded places.

"Look," said Miracle, "he's sharing his camera."

She ran ahead and gave the man her baggie of remaining coins. Buck looked proud. When he saw me he smiled. "Hello, love."

"Don't *love* me," I said.

He looked at me with puppy-dog eyes. "You still mad about this morning? I said I was sorry."

I let out a laugh. "Pfssh. No you didn't."

"Okay," he said. "I'll say it now."

He closed his eyes and held his hands as if in prayer.

"I'm not God," I said. "A simple *sorry* will do."

"I'm trying to find the right words," he said. "I want to express my regret in the sincerest way possible."

I folded my arms and leaned against the doorway of the abandoned building. "Can't wait."

Miracle copied my pose. "Me neither."

We watched as Buck's forehead furrowed in concentration. His lips were moving as if he were rehearsing a line for a school play. I rolled my eyes at Miracle. She rolled hers back at me.

When Buck opened his eyes, his face was apologetic and earnest. I actually got a bit of a lump in my throat.

He looked me in the eye. "You ready for this?"

I nodded. Miracle did too.

He cleared his throat. I waited for what I assumed would be a somewhat long and heartfelt apology. What I got was a single word:

"Soz."

Miracle burst out laughing.

I took her hand. "Let's go. I've got to get to work."

Buck walked alongside us, tucking his camera into his messenger bag. "It's how we say sorry in the U.K."

He was an idiot.

He ran his fingers through his hair.

A cute idiot.

He pointed at a coffee shop. "Who wants a donut?"

Miracle's eyes lit up.

A sneaky idiot.

"Ten minutes," I said. "Tops."

He reached for my hand. "Come on, Chicken Girl."

I swatted his hand away.

Miracle tugged on my hand. "I think he's trying to right a wrong."

I smiled. That kid was too smart for her own good.

The table we picked was etched with graffiti. Miracle sounded out the words, then turned them into a song.

Eat balls, eat balls, everybody eat balls!

She made up a dance to go with it. It was full of pelvic thrusts.

The lady behind the counter said that if I couldn't control my kid I'd have to leave.

"She's not my kid," I said. "I'm, like, sixteen."

She set our places roughly. "You're *like* sixteen? Or you *are* sixteen?"

I looked at Buck as if to say, *Is she for real?* He smiled at her and said, "Your glasses are smashing," but he should have said *smashed* because one of the lenses was missing. She was so taken by the compliment she blushed. He placed our order and called her by the name that was on her nametag. Doug. She laughed and said, "Oh, that's my coworker. I must've picked up the wrong one." They laughed like old friends. "Listen, Doug," he said. "You wouldn't mind if I borrowed your pen, would you?" She handed it over. "You're a doll." She walked away with a spring in her step.

I rolled my eyes. "Whatever that was," I said, "it won't work on me."

He flipped over a placemat. "It's called charm," he said. "Apparently I have oodles of it."

He called to Miracle, who was shaking her bootie in the front window. "Hey, Shakira. Come here, I've got a game for you."

He settled her in front of the upside down placemat and gave her the pen. "Why don't you list all the types of balls you can eat? See if you can get to ten."

Miraculously, Miracle sat quietly.

Doug returned with our watery hot chocolate and stale powdered donuts. "Here you go, hon."

It seemed Miracle and I were invisible.

Buck smiled at me from across the table. "Guess what?"

"What?"

"Chicken's my favorite."

I laughed. "Favorite what?"

"Favorite everything."

I looked into my mug. "Pfssh."

He reached out, touched the tip of my pointer finger with his. "You're cute when you splutter."

I looked away, feigning interest in Miracle's placemat. "How many do you have, Miracle?"

"One," she said. "Meat."

I casually turned my hand palm up.

"What about cheese?" I said.

I felt Buck's palm on mine.

Miracle grinned. "How about chicken?"

His hand was warm.

"How did we miss that one?"

She yawned and rested her head against my arm.

"Popcorn balls are a thing," I said. "And don't forget gum."

"How about rum and melon and matzah?" said Buck.

She sat up and started writing again. She spelled *melon* like *mellin* and *matzah* like *maza*.

I looked at Buck. He smiled and held my hand even tighter.

"I'm supposed to be working," I said.

He stuck out his bottom lip.

"Don't worry," I said. "I'll see you tonight."

I stood up. "Come on, Miracle."

I put out my hand. She slapped it away.

"Miracle!"

"I have to get to ten!" she yelled.

Doug glared at me.

"Ten was just a suggestion," I whispered. "Eight is fine."

Miracle's grip on the pen tightened. "I have to get to ten."

I laid a hand on her shoulder. "And I have to get to work."

"Then go!" she shouted. "Leave me here alone to think about balls."

I looked to Buck, unsure what to do. He got up and crouched next to her. "How about I set a timer," he said, fiddling with his watch. "Five minutes? When it goes off the game is over, no matter how far you've got. Deal?"

Miracle looked relieved. "Deal."

I sat back down. So did Buck. For the next five minutes he drew hearts into a pile of sugar he'd poured on the table. I pretended to gag.

When the timer went off, Miracle dropped her head into her arms and cried. Buck knelt next to her. "Guess what? I thought of two more."

She looked up. "You did?"

"Yep. But I must warn you, they're not everyone's cup of tea."

She perked up.

"You ready?" said Buck.

She put pen to paper.

Buck cleared his throat. "Foot and eye."

Miracle swung her leg up onto the table. "Eat my foot!"

Buck pretended to nibble it all over.

Miracle grinned. "You're funny."

Buck held out his hand. "Ready, Freddie?"

We walked hand in hand, all three of us in a row.

I'd wanted time to stand still earlier. Now I wanted it to fast-forward, to nighttime under the bridge.

When we got back to the chicken shop Mr. Chen sent me home. He said the supper rush was over so my ineffectual, inadequate, and somewhat clumsy dance moves, which were useless at the best of times, would be pointless. I saw my chicken head in a sink full of soapy water. Next to it, on the counter, was a brand-new bottle of gentle-care laundry detergent. I apologized for using whiskey. Mr. Chen said he knew that I meant well. He gave me a single chicken wing to eat on the way home.

I walked down the train tracks wondering if steam engines were still used in the forties. It was a hobby of mine, looking at today's world and imagining it then. Tonight I'd be under the bridge with Buck. If it were the forties, we'd be down at the dance hall cutting a rug. He'd be wearing a sport shirt tucked into a pair of wide-legged, high-waisted slacks and I'd be wearing a plaid skirt with a fitted angora sweater. We'd have a real gas, jitterbugging and jiving, and Buck would tell me I was a dish. At the end of the night we'd kiss on the doorstep and when I went inside I wouldn't watch videos of people being burned alive because the internet wouldn't exist yet.

I ran into Eve and a couple of derby girls on the path that led to my neighborhood.

"We were just at your house," said Ally.

"You were?" I said. "Why?"

Eve rolled her eyes. "Because friends call on other friends when they're about to have an epic night downtown."

She'd gotten her nose pierced. It looked cool. I wished I'd been with her at the piercing studio. She'd have squeezed my hand and said, *Hey, Poppy, your hand is kind of peachy too*, and I'd have laughed because having no filter is what I loved about Eve.

"How's your brother?" said Ally.

Ally's derby name was Bashin' Robbins. She was in twelfth grade and had a mad crush on Cam.

"Still gay," I said.

She snapped her fingers in disappointment. "Damn."

"I can't go out tonight," I said. "I'm meeting my boyfriend."

Eve's eyebrows shot up. "Interesting."

We leaned against the chain-link fence and chatted a bit. I told them about Buck's photography and outdoorsy good looks, and Jen (a.k.a. Cinnamon Roller) told me about their big tournament in Toronto the weekend before. Eve said, "You could have been there too, Poppy, if you weren't such a chicken."

"I'm not a chicken," I said, relieved I wasn't wearing my costume.

"Yeah you are," she said. "You're afraid to have fun."

I rolled my eyes. "Pfssh. If that was the case I wouldn't be going out with my boyfriend tonight, now would I?"

She looked me up and down, then crossed the path to hug me. "Maybe we'll see you at the rink sometime."

She kissed my cheek. "Love ya, Peach."

Except for the spot where her lips had been, my entire body felt numb.

As I walked up Churchill I thought, *This must be what regret feels like.*

Dad was channel surfing when I got home. Instead of going straight upstairs I paused in the doorway. He stopped on *Arthur*, my favorite cartoon from when I was a kid. He sang the theme song, word for word. I laughed.

He clicked from PBS to CNN. A suicide bomb had gone off in a market in Kabul. A five-year-old boy had lost his legs.

No light-up shoes for him.

⟿

I went upstairs and phoned Cam.

"Are you calling from your room?" he asked.

I sat on my bed. "Yeah."

"You couldn't walk five feet?"

I kicked off my shoes. "Nope. Say something funny."

It took him a moment.

"Birdies for sale, going cheap."

I frowned in confusion. "I don't get it."

"You will. Anyway, I gotta go. Fabian is about to call."

"Fabian, your boss?"

"Who else?" he said. "He wants to tell me about a new product line."

"But you're a floor sweeper," I said.

"For now," he said. "I think I might get promoted to cash soon."

I wanted him to stay on the phone forever. "Can't it wait until tomorrow?"

"What's the big deal, Pops? Doesn't Mr. Chen ever call you?"

"He calls me on an imaginary phone sometimes and says, 'Earth to Poppy, come in, Poppy'—but it's always during shop hours."

Cam laughed. "I gotta go. Talk to you later, Pops."

I hung up feeling unsettled.

Then I got the joke.

Cheep. Ha ha.

I googled "fit as a butcher's dog." Apparently I was healthy and physically attractive. Maybe that's what Buck had meant by "chunky." Maybe I was being too sensitive.

I put on my sailor shorts and a striped crop top. It felt good. But when I looked in the mirror I thought of The Photo and remembered the ham on the train, and suddenly I didn't feel like dressing up anymore. I wore jeans and a tee instead.

I said goodbye to Mom and Dad and went to the bridge. Buck was waiting on top with a joint in his palm.

"Want some?"

I was in the mood for obliviousness so said yes.

We sat on the grass halfway down the embankment. I smoked it like a pro. When we moved under the bridge, Thumper greeted me with a bible verse about forbidden fruits creating many jams. "Jam?" I said. "Like for toast?" Buck said his Nan made a mean marmalade. It was the funniest word in the world. Thumper said something about brain cells but all I could do was laugh.

Around nine, Lewis and Miracle showed up with dinner.

"Mama made spaghetti."

"Bloody hell," muttered Buck. "That kid's a hot mess."

I looked at her herringbone top and checkerboard leggings.

"She's not a mess," I said. "She's clatching."

Buck raised an eyebrow. "Clatching?"

"Clashing in a way that is matching," I said.

It was one of my favorite word blends. Cam made it up when I wore a dotted blouse with a floral-print skirt.

"How can you clash and match at the same time?" asked Buck.

"The same way you can eat jumbo shrimp in deafening silence," I said.

He rubbed his eyes. "I don't know what's doing my head in more—her outfit or your ramblings."

"Probably my ramblings," I said. "Because her outfit is awfully good."

I thought that was seriously funny but Buck didn't laugh.

Lewis placed the pot, paper plates, and plastic cutlery on the ground and Thumper dished out the spaghetti.

Buck grinned at me. "We can do that thing with the noodle."

I was too hungry for that. I ate my helping quickly.

"You okay?" asked Lewis. "You look a little green."

The words came out tasting sour. "I'm fine."

Miracle was in Lewis's lap, one hand clutching Gilbert, the other rubbing his head.

"I love your outfit today," I said. "Mixing big prints with small ones is really smart. It's what all the big fashion designers do."

Buck lit up another joint. "Fashion designers on crack."

"I wish you wouldn't do that here," said Lewis, nodding toward Miracle.

"Her mother's a hooker," he said. "I'm sure she's seen worse."

Lewis directed his look of disgust at me, as if I had been the one that had said it. I felt even sicker.

I glared at Buck. "What the hell was that?"

He shrugged like he had no idea what I was talking about.

I turned to Miracle, to apologize on Buck's behalf, but Thumper was already distracting her with a game of Trouble. "Who wants to play?"

Buck was too high and I was too sick but everyone else said yes. The popping sound hurt my head. Buck offered me the joint. I waved it away.

"I think I'm going to be sick."

His eyes were half closed as he waved a hand through the air. "The river's over there, love."

The thought of my puke running downstream made me feel sicker.

"Where do you guys go," I asked, "when you have to go?"

Buck took a long draw. "There's a loo in the drop-in center."

My stomach was churning. "Where?"

He pointed toward the sky. "Up."

Lewis left the Trouble game in a rage. "Jesus Christ, Buck."

He helped me up and wrapped an arm around my waist. We walked slowly up the embankment.

"Won't be long," he said. "Hang in there . . . thirty more seconds."

Pavement turned to floor turned to blurry toilet bowl. With Lewis's arms around my waist I hurled. My whole body convulsed. I was shaking from head to toe. He held my hair out of my face and when I was done he brought me to a bench. He soaked paper towels in cool water and put them on my forehead. I was going to say sorry but said "again" instead. He whisked me to the stall and I retched up every last thing in my stomach and then I retched some more.

Back on the bench I closed my eyes. He gave me water.

"Sorry," I said. "That was gross."

"Don't apologize. I care for my dad. I've seen worse."

"What's wrong with your dad?"

"He's dying."

"I'm sorry."

My stomach started churning again. "I must have the flu."

"Yeah," he said. "The weed flu."

"Can I put my head on your shoulder?"

"Go ahead."

He was wearing a T-shirt with the sleeves rolled up. My cheek rested against his bare skin.

"How did you meet Thumper?" I asked.

"I met him at a walk-in clinic with my dad. They were both there for pain relief. Dad and Thumper got to talking. When Dad found out that Thumper lived under the Fifth Street bridge, he made me bring him some food and blankets. I've been going there ever since."

"And Miracle?"

"She lives next door. Her mom helps out with my dad sometimes. I return the favor by watching Miracle in the evenings. We used to just hang out at my place, but then Dad got too sick. When the overnight caregiver comes, we leave. It's a nice break, you know? From the doom and gloom."

"Yes," I said. "I know what you mean."

He looked at me questioningly. I didn't offer anything more.

"So you live on Victoria too," I said.

He nodded. "Yep."

"You never mentioned it that night you dropped Miracle home," I said.

"You mean that night you gave me a history lesson on wartime houses?" he said. "I could hardly get a word in edgewise."

I managed a laugh.

"Wait now," I said. "If you live in my neighborhood—"

He cut me off.

"I don't go to Pearson High because my dad prefers the student-teacher ratio at Westvale."

I smiled. "Are you a mind reader?"

"Yes," he said. "And yours is constantly churning."

So was my stomach.

I closed my eyes, let my mind churn some more. "Miracle wants to be a backup dancer."

There must have been a hint of judgment in my voice.

"So?" he said.

"She could be so much more."

"Don't overthink it," he said. "She's only six."

We sat for another few minutes.

"She still sucks her thumb."

"It gives her comfort," he said.

I reached up, brushed my fingers along his shaved bits. "So does rubbing your head."

"Her dad had a brush cut," he said. "She figures this is what it feels like."

"She said he died," I said.

He nodded. "Afghanistan. She was just a baby."

My heart sunk. "Poor thing."

After a long silence I said, "I'm ready to go back."

We walked like turtles. No, snails. Buck jumped up when he saw me.

"Are you okay?"

Lewis shot him a look. "She's fine."

Buck slid his arm between us. "Thanks, mate," he said. "I can take over from here."

He opened up his sleeping bag. I crawled in.

He propped himself on his elbow. "I'm sorry, Pidge."

"For what?"

"Chasing hens around a farmyard while you, the love of my life, got put in the dog pound."

I managed a smile.

"I am a mangy, no-good mongrel," he said. "I knew you were sick. And I kept getting high anyway."

I shrugged. "Nobody's perfect."

He leaned over, kissed my nose. "You're pretty bloody close."

"Pfssh. I'm the most flawed person I know."

"How so?"

"For one thing, I'm a chicken."

"That's your job," he said. "How is that a flaw?"

"I use it as a way to hide."

"From what?"

"The world."

"Why?"

"It's an overwhelming place."

He pulled me close and recited Tramp's speech about life off the leash, about the world being a place where two dogs could have fun and adventure. He said, "Don't fence yourself in, Pidge."

I held his hand. "I'm not the love of your life, you know."

"Not yet," he said. "But you could be."

～

The potential love of my life fell asleep so Lewis became my walking buddy. We brought Miracle home first. It was twelve-thirty and she cried at being woken. She whimpered in Lewis's arms the whole way and when he delivered her to her mother, a petite blonde with striking green eyes, she said, "Mama, why can't you work in the day?"

The crankiness over the Eat Balls List was just beginning to dawn on me.

Lewis pointed to a house next to Miracle's. "Home sweet home."

It was a Plan 47-11. I thought of the dying man inside. I wanted to hug my parents.

We walked from Victoria to Churchill. Lewis asked why I'd grown so silent.

"Her mother's so young," I said. "And so pretty."

He bumped his shoulder into mine and smiled. "Would it be easier for you if she was old and ugly?"

He was challenging my thinking, in a gentle way.

"The whole thing," I said, "it's such a shame."

"Agreed," he said. "But young and pretty has nothing to do with it."

We walked for a long time in silence. When my house appeared in the distance I said, "You know, I think I might be quick to judge sometimes."

He grinned. "Ya think?"

I bumped him gently with my shoulder. "You know, you're pretty wise for a sixteen-year-old."

He smiled. "That's because I went to the school of hard knocks."

"Really?" I said. "And here I thought you went to Westvale."

He laughed. "I'm not wise. I've just been through stuff, you know? Sometimes people jump to conclusions about me, so I try not to jump to conclusions about them. I try to look at things from all angles."

"I wish I could be like that," I said.

"Maybe you need to hang out with me more," he said. "You never know, all that so-called wisdom might rub off on you."

When we reached the bottom of Churchill he said, "See you tomorrow night?"

"Yeah," I said. "Probably."

But it wasn't a probably, it was a yes, not just for that night but for the one after that and the one after that and the one after that.

It was a yes to something new.

CHAPTER FOUR

On a random July morning, instead of grabbing a handful of cereal and retreating to my room, I sat with my parents for breakfast. Mom and Dad chatted away. It was nice.

Dad told us about a job he had over in Falconridge. He said the house was open concept with six bedrooms, four bathrooms, two living spaces, a billiards room, and a home theater. He said the homeowners wanted the whole house painted steel grey. He said that he and his crew were only halfway through and it looked horrible.

I said, "Just goes to show, you don't need walls to live in a prison."

They knew exactly what I meant. We all loved our closed-plan home.

Mom told us about a kid at school who had made her a thank-you card because she gave bigger helpings than the other lunch ladies. She said, "He taped macaroni noodles to the construction paper because mac and cheese is his favorite."

I said, "There's this little girl who hangs around the shop. Maybe she goes to your school. Her name's Miracle. She's pretty entertaining."

Mom spooned some sugar into her coffee. "Miracle Melendez? Cute little thing. Incredibly polite for her age."

I sighed with relief, grateful it was politeness she was known for.

Mom took a sip of her coffee and let out an *aaaah*. "So," she said with a grin. "How's the boyfriend?"

I almost choked on my Honeycombs.

I was going to kill Cam.

"He's . . . fine?"

"Fine as in okay?" said Dad. "Or fine as in 'Damn, that boy is fine'?"

I stood up. "And on that note . . ."

Mom laughed and caught my hand as I walked by. "Invite him over sometime. We'd love to meet him."

He'd charm the pants right off them.

"Sure," I said. "As long as Dad doesn't talk."

Dad zipped his lips.

Mom's hand felt warm in mine.

As I walked upstairs I decided that Honeycombs tasted better from a bowl.

When I arrived at work, Miracle was doing a dance routine for the customers. Mr. Chen cheered her along.

"Don't encourage her," I said. "She thinks she's going to be famous."

He looked me up and down. "You always did strike me as a Negative Nellie."

I preened my feathers. "I prefer Pessimistic Poppy, thank you very much."

"Everyone should be allowed to dream," he said. "I came to Canada with twenty dollars in my pocket. Now look at me! I singlehandedly run a successful business! And I'm the president of the Downtown Business Association."

I'd never thought of him that way before. As someone who'd come from somewhere else, who had to start over. To me he was Mr. Chen, successful local businessman, pillar of the community, crotchety old man.

I put on my costume and went outside. I hopped and I skipped and I jumped. I shimmy-shimmy-kicked and I wiggled my butt. I even attempted a pirouette.

Twenty dollars. That's what he had. Twenty bucks to his name. He'd built a business from scratch, all on his own. The least I could do was promote it.

I wondered for the first time about his private life. Did he have a wife? Kids? I knew nothing about him. I felt bad about that. Maybe I needed to make more connections with the people around me. After all, wasn't that what Thumper said it was all about?

A car full of teenagers drove by and one of them threw an empty beer bottle at my head.

It was hard being a chicken.

Before my shift ended Miracle told me that it was Lewis's birthday. I wanted to get him a little something but didn't know what. It was the connection thing again. I needed to work on that.

After work I went to the nicer part of downtown. In a high-end skateboard shop I found the perfect gift—a Converse high-top keychain.

I made a point of walking by Bliss before heading home. I looked in the window to see Cam, not sweeping the floors as I had expected but sitting in a chair getting a head massage. The person giving it looked to be in his early thirties. He was a beefy guy with slicked-back hair and a neatly trimmed beard. He wore a fitted white T-shirt and blue jeans and his arms were covered with tattoos. I had a bad feeling it was Fabian.

It was 7:25. Cam would be off soon. I sat at a bus stop and waited.

At 7:38 he strutted toward me in his signature runway-stomp style.

"Next time you want to spy on me, Pops, you might want to ditch the giant chicken costume."

"I was in the area," I said.

He started down the sidewalk. "Yeah. Right."

I waddled beside him. "So. How was the head massage?"

"Oh, for God's sake, Poppy. How else am I going to learn the ropes?"

"I'm worried about you, Cam."

"I have a job," he said. "A nice boss. Why do you see negativity in everything?"

I was surprised by the wobble in my voice. "Because I'm a chicken," I said. "A big scaredy-cat chicken."

He stopped walking and turned to face me. "Come here, Pops."

He opened his arms extra wide. I walked into them and breathed in his goodness.

"Did you know," I said, wrapping my wings around him, "that when you went to boxing camp when we were ten, I went to your closet and stuck my nose on all of your shirts?"

"Good God, Poppy. What is wrong with you?"

"It was because you have a smell. Everyone does. And yours is nice. I wanted you with me, so I breathed you in as much as I could."

"Oh, Pops," he said. "I'll always be with you. Even when I'm not."

I smiled. As if everything was okay. But Cam knew better.

"What are you afraid of?" he asked.

"Bad things happening."

"Good things happen too, Popsicle."

"Yes," I said. "But the bad always outweighs the good."

"Did anything bad happen today?" he asked.

"I got hit in the head with a beer bottle."

"Anything else?"

Fabian's creepy hands were all over your head.

"Not really."

"Anything good happen?" he asked.

I thought for a moment. "I had breakfast with Mom and Dad. That was kind of nice."

"Anything else?"

"Mr. Chen actually motivated me instead of berating me. Oh, and I bought a birthday present for one of my friends from the bridge."

Cam held up one finger with his left hand, four with his right. "Looks to me like the good is outweighing the bad."

I pointed to his right hand. "That should be three."

"No," he said. "Four. Reddit took down ISccFatPeople today."

I grinned. "Really?"

He nodded. "It was free speech versus hate speech for a while there, but in the end they decided it violated their new anti-harassment policy."

"Well, duh," I said.

98

We walked wing in arm the rest of the way. We didn't separate until we got to the landing.

"Later, Scaredy-Cat Chicken."

I went to my room and went online.

The Photo was gone.

I didn't feel scared anymore.

CHAPTER FIVE

There was a balloon bouquet under the bridge but the mood was gloomy and dark.

Buck greeted me with a kiss.

"Hello, my little chicken nugget."

He reeked of alcohol.

I looked to Lewis.

"Ignore him. He's drunk."

Buck reached out, poked my stomach. "What's wrong, Pillsbury? Cat got your tongue?"

My insides shook.

"You were supposed to giggle," said Buck. "The Pillsbury Doughboy giggles when he's poked in his wibbly-wobbly belly."

"It's the alcohol talking," said Thumper. "Don't take it to heart."

"He'll go back to normal soon," said Miracle. "He always does."

Lewis sat near the fire. "Come sit with me, Poppy."

"No," said Buck. "She'll sit with me."

Lewis held out his hand. I took it.

My voice quivered. "What's happening right now?"

"He goes on a bender sometimes," said Lewis. "Don't worry. He'll be back to his normal annoying self in a few days."

Buck almost fell into the fire trying to sit next to it. "Hey, Poppy. Why did the chicken cross the road?"

My shock quickly turned to anger.

"I don't know," I said. "To punch its boyfriend in the face?"

"No," he said. "To get to the udder side."

"I think you mean *cow*," said Miracle. "Why did the *cow* cross the road?"

"How am I supposed to know?" he said. "Do I look like a fucking shepherd?"

Lewis stood up. "Watch your mouth, Buck."

Buck laughed. "Or what?"

"Or I'll punch your face in."

"You probably could," said Buck. "You look pretty strong, considering."

I frowned. "What's that supposed to mean?"

Lewis took a step forward. "It means he's an asshole."

I tugged on his hand. "Sit down, Lewis. He's not worth it."

Buck stumbled off to his sleeping bag. I was glad.

Miracle gave Lewis a large piece of poster board folded in half. "It's the world's biggest birthday card," she said. "And I made it!"

Every inch was covered in colored balloons.

"Thanks, Miracle. I love it."

Thumper passed him a Folgers coffee can. Lewis peeled back the rubber lid and looked inside.

"It's a little over four hundred dollars," said Thumper. "To help get you and your dad to Toronto for the operation."

Lewis's eyes filled with tears. "How did you raise this?"

"I asked some local business owners for donations. Mr. Chen was very generous. I panhandled a bit too. Some kind soul put in a hundred-dollar bill."

"And I added three dollars and forty-five cents," said Miracle.

Lewis stared into the can. I didn't recognize his voice for the shaking. "My dad's been saving for so long," he said. "For the train fares, for the accommodation during the recovery. This will really help."

I was happy for Lewis but confused too. If Lewis's dad was terminal I couldn't see how an operation would save him.

Miracle squeezed in between Lewis and me. She had three long skewers and a bag of marshmallows. "Mama said we should celebrate."

Thumper opened his bible. "'If we are lucky, we'll all experience a rebirth. Be it physical or emotional. Or both.'"

Sometimes Thumper's bible really confused me.

We sat around the fire telling jokes. I tried to relax but my heart was still stinging from the Doughboy comment.

Buck stared at me from across the platform. He picked up his camera and took a picture. I said, "Don't you have a home to go to?" It was a mean thing to say to a homeless person but I figured he deserved it. He responded by aiming the camera at Lewis. "Hey, Wooden Boy. Say cheese."

Lewis tensed up beside me. I reached out, covered his fist with my hand, rubbing my thumb across his Pinocchio tattoo.

Miracle hopped up and struck a pose. "Gorgonzola!"

Buck took the shot, then passed her the camera. "Now you take one of me."

He took a moment to get in position. "Look familiar, Poppy?"

All at once he crushed me.

"All I need is a hamburger," he said. "And maybe that dishrag you're wearing on your head."

The others looked confused.

I stood up. "You're horrible, Buck."

I turned to go.

"Poppy," said Lewis. "Wait."

But I didn't wait. I ran. Down by the river and through

a tangle of bushes. I ran until I came to a clearing. There I sat, shaking.

He ate footballs and eyeballs. He shared his camera and had oodles of charm.

I lay back on the ground and stared at the sky.

I heard rustling, hoped it was a bear. I hoped it would eat me. But it wasn't a bear—it was Thumper, struggling to get through the shrubbery.

He stood above me, winded.

"You were wrong," I said. "Alcohol can't talk. Only wankers can. And plonkers and pillocks and tossers and prats." I sat up. "I told him something and he threw it back in my face."

Thumper eased himself down next to me and picked a twig out of my hair.

"Look at me," I said. "I'm a mess."

"Don't worry," he said. "Moses was a basket case too."

I laughed until the stars blurred.

He put his arm around me and I sobbed into his leather vest.

"Just when I thought that good outweighed bad," I said, "Buck had to go and tip the scales."

He wiped a tear off my cheek with one of his bony fingers. "A wise man once said, 'The battle line between good and evil runs through the heart of every man.'"

"If that's the case, Buck's losing the war."

Thumper smiled. "It's not always easy, you know, getting to the other side."

"Don't I know it," I said. "I'm a chicken, remember? Apparently it's my main goal."

He laughed. "Well, just remember: Obstacles do not block the path. They *are* the path."

I rolled my eyes. "Great."

He patted my hand. "Let's go back, Poppy."

"You go," I said. "I'm staying here."

"Not at this time of night you're not. It's dangerous."

I helped him up and we headed back through the bushes together.

I stumbled over a rock. He grabbed my arm. We walked the rest of the way like that, him thinking he was supporting me when it was me who was supporting him.

When Buck saw me he opened his arms. "I knew you'd come back."

"I came back," I said, "because Thumper said it was dangerous."

Buck laughed. "He should know. Have a google of those letters on his arm."

I looked at Thumper. He looked away.

Lewis stood up. "Need a walking buddy?"

I nodded. "Yes."

He settled Thumper next to Miracle. "I'll be back for her soon."

Thumper laid a protective hand on Miracle's shoulder as she slept.

He was the loveliest man I'd ever met.

Lewis and I walked up the embankment. When we got to the top I showed him the photo on my phone.

"That's beautiful," he said.

"Someone posted it on a subreddit called ISeeFatPeople," I said. "They photoshopped a burger in my hand."

"That's horrible," he said.

"Buck thought it was hysterical."

"Buck's an asshole."

We walked down Fifth Street toward Elgin.

"The whole thing," I said. "It's changed my outlook on life. People really suck."

He bumped his shoulder gently into mine. "Not all people."

We walked past the shops on Elgin. The light above Chen Chicken was on. I wondered what Mr. Chen was doing. Probably thinking up insults for me. More likely, though, he was catching up on the paperwork he never got to during the day.

"I'm sorry about Buck," I said. "He ruined your birthday."

Lewis shrugged. "I care more about how he hurt you."

"Wow," I said. "We've come a long way, haven't we?"

"What do you mean?"

"Well, my first impression kind of sucked. That whole 'you don't look homeless' thing didn't go down too well."

Lewis pulled a piece of paper out of his back pocket.

"This kind of won me over."

It was the note I'd put in the snub tub.

I smiled. "I only said that I liked the way you cuffed your Levi's over your Chuck Taylors."

When we got to the railway tracks he said, "You can ask if you want. I don't mind."

"Ask what?"

"What the operation is for."

"I figured it was for your dad."

He smiled. "I wish."

"So who's it for?"

He stopped walking. "Me."

My heart sunk. "Are you sick?"

"Ha! Yeah. Sick of being trapped in the wrong body."

"What do you mean?"

He looked me in the eye. "I'm hoping, someday, to get bottom surgery."

"What, like butt implants?"

He laughed. "No."

I remembered Thumper's words about rebirth.

"Oh," I said. "I get it."

"Surprised?"

"A bit."

I looked at his muscular chest. "So I guess you've had top surgery already?"

"Last year. Want to see?"

I nodded.

He pulled me into the light of a lamppost and lifted his shirt.

"It looks amazing."

"I was on testosterone for all of tenth grade," he said. "And I work out a lot."

"I think you're very brave," I said.

He shrugged. "It wasn't a choice. It's who I'm meant to be."

"So what was your name before?" I asked.

He cringed. "That's kind of a rude question."

"Is it?" I said. "I'm sorry."

"It's just . . . it's so irrelevant, you know? I'm Lewis now. That's what matters."

I thought about that for a few seconds.

"I can see that," I said. "It'd be like if your dog died and you got a new one and everyone was like, 'Hey, this dog sucks, your old one was way better.'"

He laughed. "Um. Actually no. It's not like that at all."

I rubbed my chin. "I think I might need to think on this a bit longer."

Lewis smiled. "It's a lot to get your head around if you don't live it."

I looked into his face. "I'm sorry you were born with bits you didn't want."

He tapped the end of my nose with his finger. "You're adorkable."

I smiled. "My brother would like that word."

"You have a brother?"

That's when I remembered. I pulled the keychain out of my pocket. "I don't know much about you either," I said. "But I thought you might like this."

I passed it to him. "Happy birthday."

He held it like it was a precious jewel.

"I hope you get your bottom surgery," I said. "So you can be complete."

"It's not about being complete," he said. "I mean, plenty of people choose *not* to get surgery and they're just as complete as anyone else."

I had a lot to learn from Lewis.

We kept walking. He swung his new keychain round and round on his finger. We talked the whole way home. I told him I had a birthmark on my thigh and won a pie-eating contest once. He told me he dressed as SpongeBob for Halloween three years in a row and he broke his arm when he was five. We both loved Honeycombs.

Cam was in bed but awake. I plunked down next to him.

"What's up, Popsicle?"

"Buck called me the Pillsbury Doughboy."

"Want me to go give him a knuckle sandwich?"

I almost said yes. I would have loved to see Cam throw a punch again.

"He's such a stupid asshole," I said.

"Yeah," he said. "He's a real"—he paused for effect—"ignoranus."

"Ha," I said. "Good one."

I laid my head on his shoulder.

He was scrolling through his Instagram account. Every photo a close-up of his beautifully made-up face.

"Is that a new phone?"

He nodded. "Fabian got it for me. Mine was scratched."

"Why would your boss buy you a new phone?"

"He said it was a bonus. Doesn't Mr. Chen ever give you a bonus?"

"He gave me a chicken wing once."

"See? Every job has its perks."

We lay side by side, our breath synchronized and getting deeper. I reached for his pinkie. "Say something funny, Cam."

"When it comes to illegal drug use, cocaine is where I draw the line."

I laughed.

Together, we slept until morning.

CHAPTER SIX

The next day the whole thing replayed in my mind.

The Pillsbury Doughboy giggles when he's poked in his wibbly-wobbly belly.

Look familiar, Poppy?

Have a google of those letters on his arm.

I pictured it—the four letters above the motorcycle tattoo.

I opened my laptop.

Whatever it was, it wouldn't come as a surprise. Nothing did anymore.

I typed them in.

S.O.A.R.

Results included a village in Wales, an aviation unit in the U.S. army, and a song by Christina Aguilera.

I added *motorcycle* to my search. The first result was a biker club.

Sons of Aryan Resistance.

I liked Thumper. He'd rewritten the Bible. He made it nicer.

> *Mission:* to patrol the streets and cleanse them of
> undesirables
> *Undesirables:* racial minorities, immigrants, and
> sexual degenerates

I felt sick.

Maybe he was part of that aviation unit. Or was Christina Aguilera's number one fan.

I watched footage of them in action. Boots on heads and red, red blood.

Maybe that's why he's called Thumper.

I got dressed. I had to go out but I didn't know where.

I walked down Churchill wishing for that thirty-second loop of Miracle and me walking hand in hand down James Street. Clip-clop, flash, flash, repeat.

Ralph was sweeping the sidewalk in front of his house. He waved me over.

"A young couple just moved into number thirty-two," he said. "They're putting on an addition. It's going to ruin the look of the whole street."

Normally, I'd have cared. Normally, I'd have stood with him and ranted and raved. I'd have said that renovations compromise the integrity of historic homes, that modernization strips wartime houses of their quaintness and charm. But suddenly, I didn't care. "Oh well," I said. "C'est la vie."

I walked to Victoria Road and knocked on the door of Plan 47-11.

"Want to go for a walk?"

Lewis nodded. "Give me a sec."

I heard a woman's voice. "You go. Don't worry. Have fun."

We walked along the tracks, just as we had the night before.

"Did you know," I said, "that the royal train carried King George and Queen Elizabeth down these very tracks in 1939?"

He smiled. "And you know this because . . ."

"I googled steam trains in the forties and saw a photo."

"Wow," he said. "You really *are* obsessed."

I smiled. "It was a great era."

He didn't look convinced. "Really? How so?"

"Well, first of all," I said, "there was no internet."

He looked thoughtful. "Fair enough. What else?"

"Things were just . . . I don't know . . . simpler."

"Really?" he said. "There was a war going on. How is that simple?"

I sighed. "Because right was right and wrong was wrong. I mean, nobody questioned whether Hitler was breaking any harassment guidelines or debated hate speech versus free speech."

He stopped walking. "Whoa. Are you serious?"

"I'm just saying. Back then, there was no ambiguity. Things were pretty clear-cut."

"So let me get this right. You would rather live during World War II when millions and millions of people died because living in the world today puts you at risk of cyber-bullying?"

"Well, it sounds stupid when you say it like that."

"That's because it *is* stupid."

I sighed. "The war was terrible. I know that. But people came together over it, you know? It was all for one and one for all. It was a very empowering time for women too."

"Until the war ended and they were barefoot and pregnant in the kitchen again."

"Geez, Lewis. Why are you being so difficult? This is supposed to be easier with you."

He frowned. "What does that mean?"

"Buck's an arsehole. But you . . . you're a good guy."

"Which means what?" he said. "Everything I do should be perfect?"

"No, that's not what I—"

"Maybe I should put on an army uniform and march off to war or say, *Golly gee willikers, Poppy, you sure are swell* to everything you say."

"That's not what I'm saying—"

"Life is a mixture of good and bad, Poppy. It was then, it is now, and it always will be."

"Why are you so angry?"

"I'm not angry. I'm frustrated. Your thinking is really warped."

The gravel next to the tracks crunched under our feet.

"The thing is," I said, "my issues wouldn't have existed if I lived in the forties."

"And mine would have been shameful," he said. "I'd have been unhappy my whole life."

My heart quivered.

We heard the *ding-ding-ding* of the commuter train in the distance. We moved well away from the tracks. When the train passed I could see Chen Chicken between two buildings that backed onto the railway line. Mr. Chen was outside his shop chatting enthusiastically with the other shop owners. Lewis bumped his shoulder into mine. "Just think, if this was the forties you probably wouldn't have a job as a giant chicken."

"Yeah," I said. "Bummer."

When the train was gone we turned back toward home. We veered off the tracks and onto Richmond Street. Lewis went into a corner store and came out with a Popsicle. He broke it in half.

"Pineapple," I said. "My favorite."

Back on the tracks I said, "I'm sorry about how your life would be in the forties."

"Don't worry," he said. "I don't plan on taking a trip back in time."

The icy cold felt nice on my lips. "Did you know that the word *Popsicle* is a word blend? The inventor's kids came up with it. Pop's icicles. Popsicles!"

He tapped the end of my nose with his ice pop. "Have I told you you're adorkable?"

I wiped my nose with the back of my hand and wondered if it was unbecoming.

At the bottom of Churchill we said goodbye.

"Will I see you again?" he asked. "Under the bridge?"

I shook my head. "Not while Buck's around."

"Maybe we can go for a walk again?"

I smiled. "I'd like that."

When I got home Mom was hanging a sign in our kitchen that said *Homemade with love. In other words, I licked the spoon and kept using it.*

She looked down at me from the stepstool. "Hilarious, huh?"

I didn't get it. Was she trying to say that spit equaled love? If so, my *pfssh*es were basically saliva hugs.

"How's the boyfriend?" she said.

"Nonexistent right now."

"Oh. I'm sorry, hon."

She passed me a package of Oreos the way she'd pass me a Band-Aid for a cut.

"Here. This'll help."

I took one out and twisted it in half.

Mom sat beside me. "Eve called today."

I scraped the icing off with my teeth. "She did?"

Mom nodded. "I thought you'd be back on the team, now that it's summer."

I'd told her I left because I was falling behind on my studies.

I wasn't sure what to say. Luckily, Cam burst in with an announcement.

"I've been promoted!"

"To what?" I asked. "Senior hair sweeper?"

He shot me a look. "Head of guest services."

Mom was impressed. "Good for you, Cam!"

"I still sweep," he said. "But Fabe says I'll be mostly on cash, dealing with customers."

Fabe.

I stood up. "I have to get ready for work."

"Have fun sweating your ass off in your chicken costume," said Cam.

"Don't worry," I said. "I will."

I hated it when there was tension between us. I went upstairs and texted an apology for the senior sweeper comment. He texted back: *No prob. Love you, Popsicle.* He signed off with six *x*'s and six *o*'s.

➳

I sat on the barbershop bench with Miracle. Her little body was pressed up close to mine. I didn't feel sad but I didn't feel happy either. The sun was shining and she'd just placed a random kiss on my feathery elbow. It wasn't bad and it wasn't good, it just was.

"Guess what?" she said.

"What?"

"I went to James Street today. MaJonna taught me to twerk."

"I told you to stay away from that neighborhood."

"He sang 'Like a Virgin' and now I know all the words."

I sighed. "Great."

"MaJonna taught me some cool moves," she said. "Want me to teach them to you?"

"Sure," I said. "Why not?"

She showed me how to do the Roger Rabbit and the Running Man. A couple of drunks joined in. Someone yelled, "Go Chicken, it's your birthday" from a passing car. Another mascot, Willie the Wiener from Hawt Dawgs, challenged me to a dance-off. A crowd formed. The wiener won. The shift went by fast. When it was over I asked Mr. Chen if he wanted me to stay longer.

He was suspicious. "Why?"

Because if I went home I'd watch videos of S.O.A.R.

"Because I'm broke and need to earn a few bucks."

He looked me up and down. "You always did strike me as a spendthrift."

"Maybe I can help in the kitchen," I said.

"You? In the kitchen? I want satisfied customers, Poppy Flower! Not dead ones!"

All of a sudden I felt drained.

"I don't want to argue with you, Mr. Chen."

I picked up my head and walked to the door.

"Poppy," he said. "Wait."

I turned around. "Yeah?"

He nodded at the till. "You can work the cash."

I let myself smile. "Really?"

"Why not?" he said. "You're probably good with money— seeing how you spend it like it's going out of style."

We worked well together, him cooking the chicken and me selling it.

"See?" I said, during a quiet moment. "Isn't this better than you doing it all yourself?"

He was about to answer when the phone rang. I picked it up quickly. "Chen Chicken. Poppy speaking. How may I be of service?"

He rolled his eyes but I could tell he was impressed with my professionalism.

It was a great night and it only got better. When we closed up shop I walked outside to see not just Chen Chicken but the whole of Elgin Street lit up in white fairy lights.

It was all for one and one for all.

Just like the good old days.

⟜

A couple of weeks went by. I worked extra shifts to keep busy. Miracle asked if I'd ever forgive Buck and I said no, third chances were for suckers.

Lewis and I went on occasional walks. We talked about everything: his dad, who was getting weaker by the day, and my Cam, whose new job had me worried.

We talked about Miracle too. "If she's twerking at age six," I said, "imagine how provocative she'll be when she's older." Lewis said, "Your Rosie the Riveter was pretty sexy. And what about those pinup girls?" I explained that pinup girls owned their sexuality at a time when they were expected to act demure. "In my opinion," I said, "they are symbols of feminism." He said, "Maybe Miracle will be a symbol of feminism too."

These were the deep conversations I had with Lewis.

I didn't miss Buck very much.

But Thumper? Lewis said he was doing fine but my heart still pained to think of him.

⟶

One day, early in August, Buck showed up at Chen Chicken. I put up an ice shield in all directions.

"Take your head off, Poppy."

He had an expensive bouquet of flowers in his hand. I shook my head.

"Come on. Please?"

"You made fun of me."

"I was plastered."

"You were nasty."

"I'm a twonk. I don't know why I said the things that I said."

"Go away. I'm working."

"I want you to come with me."

"Come with you where?"

"I want you to see the streets. Through my eyes."

"Why?"

"Because maybe then you'd understand me."

"You're going to blame the streets now, are you?" I said. "For being an asshole?"

"Just give me a chance. Please?"

"I'm working."

"After work."

"No."

"Come on, Pidge. You can help me deliver these flowers to Miracle's mom."

"They're for Miracle's mom?"

"I want to thank her for the home cooking she sends under the bridge."

He brought the flowers to his nose. "I also wanted to show her that not all men are tossers."

I thawed a bit beneath my costume.

"So," he said. "Will you come?"

It was like Lewis said, life is a mixture of good and bad. I couldn't expect him to be perfect.

"I'm off in an hour."

⟫

Miracle's mom was skin and bones. The forget-me-nots matched the veins in her arms.

"Thanks, Buck. They're lovely."

She was lovely too—despite her pale and haggard appearance.

Miracle's house was the same as Ralph's—Plan 47-4. We sat in the living room, which faced the street. Portraits filled the wall, mostly of Miracle, but of a man in uniform too. Miracle followed my gaze. "That's Papa."

She pointed to the words on a plaque underneath. *Corporal Mateo Melendez. Royal Canadian Regiment.*

Miracle's mom made a whimper. Buck left me on the loveseat and moved to the couch. He put an arm around her. He was the nicest asshole I'd ever met.

There were upholstery buttons on the arm of the love-seat. Miracle straddled it and held one in each hand. She was twisting them—counterclockwise with her left hand, clockwise with her right. She turned them until they had no give. I waited for them to pop. "A social worker came today," she said. "They might take me away."

Buck patted the space next to him. "Come here, love." She wiggled in close and stuck her thumb in her mouth. I stayed where I was, useless as always.

Miracle's mom wiped her eyes. "I'd clean toilets all day long if I could. But no one wants an ex-addict in their house, around their valuables."

She looked at the portrait on the wall. "I've made a mess of things. He'd be so disappointed."

I was worried for Miracle. Who would buy her clothes that clatched?

"No one is going anywhere," said Buck. "Everything's going to be okay."

I wasn't sure why he was saying these things. Miracle *could* get taken away. Stuff like that happened all the time.

"Now," said Buck, "as we say in England, a nice cup of tea solves everything."

Miracle's mom smiled. "I'll put the kettle on."

Buck caught my eye. He made Gilbert the rabbit dance on his knee. A smile formed around Miracle's thumb. I was no longer a block of ice, I was a puddle.

Buck steadied the lens. "Give us a smile, Tommy."

The man with the syringe in his arm glanced up. He pushed the plunger with his eyes on the camera, a euphoric look on his face.

He threw the needle on the ground. Buck took a picture of that too.

We walked down an alley. Buck took close-ups of brick.

More shots: rugged faces, strewn garbage, a dandelion growing from a sidewalk crack.

We ended up on an old railway bridge, deserted and covered in grass. We sat on the wall, our legs dangling over the edge. Buck zoomed in on the syringe in the man's arm. "I see a lot of nasty things, out here on the streets. I'm drawn to document them. I don't know why. Mad, isn't it?"

"Maybe you do it," I said, "because it makes you feel more alive."

He smiled. "See? I knew you'd understand me if you saw the streets through my eyes."

"I don't know about that," I said. "You're still a mystery."

"Me? Nah. I'm an open book. Ask me anything."

"Why do you live under the bridge?"

"My mom turfed me out."

"Why?"

"She caught me with weed and now she thinks I'm a crazy drug addict."

He took my hand. "Anything else?"

"How come sometimes you're incredibly nice and other times you're a complete asshole?"

"Because drinking turns me into a nasty plonker."

"What about when you're sober?"

He shrugged. "I guess I have a natural inclination for assholeness."

I laughed. "I guess you do."

I linked my arm through his and laid my head on his shoulder. "Buck? Do you think Miracle will get taken away?"

His brow furrowed. "Not if I can help it."

"You really care about them, don't you?"

"Her mom and me, we have this weird connection."

I was surprised. "Really?"

"Yeah," he said. "We're both screwups."

They were an unlikely pair, the fresh-faced Brit and the ex-druggie prostitute.

"She told me she was an addict when she met Mateo," he said. "He changed her life, took her away from it all. But when he died, she threw it all away. She blew their savings on drugs, then prostituted herself to support her habit. Now she does it to support Miracle."

"That's sad," I said.

And it was.

But Miracle.

Sweet, mischievous Miracle.

How was she not enough to turn things around?

Buck stood up, took a key out of his pocket. "Come with me?"

"Where?"

"I'm watching a friend's flat while he's away."

We walked hand in hand, far from the James Street area to the trendier side of the downtown core. Above a bistro was a loft-style apartment filled with sleek furniture and stunning artwork.

"This place is amazing."

"Isaac's an art collector. He's shown interest in my photos. You never know, I might make it big someday."

One of the kitchen walls was brick, and the other was filled with a floor-to-ceiling painting of a naked woman. A center island was surrounded by chrome barstools.

Shiny pots and pans hung above it from a wooden rack.

He took a bottle of wine out of the fridge. "Care to join me?"

"I thought alcohol turned you into a nasty plonker?"

"I'll only have one," he said. He held up three fingers. "Scout's honor."

He grabbed two glasses from a cupboard. We went up a swirly iron staircase. At the top was a bedroom loft. Buck poured two glasses of wine and patted the bed.

"What if your friend comes back?"

"He's in New York."

"You should ask him if you could stay here with him," I said. "So you won't have to sleep under the bridge."

Buck fluffed the pillows against the headboard. "Nah. It's a gorgeous place but Isaac's a bit of a wanker. He's one of these blokes who's totally full of himself, you know?"

I sat on top of the covers. The wine tasted bad but I drank it anyway, half the bottle. The ceiling was bordered with fancy trim and the light that hung from it was wrought iron with six arms and candle-like bulbs.

I pointed to it. "Is that a candelabra or a chandelier?"

Buck took a joint out of the bedside table. "How would I know? I'm as common as muck."

"Maybe it's a candelier," I said. "Or a chandelabra."

He lit up. "Or maybe it's just a light hanging from a ceiling."

He passed me the joint.

"Did you know you can inhale and exhale at the same time?" I said. "It's called circular breathing."

"You mean it's not called inexhaling? Or exinhaling?"

I copied his accent. "Are you taking the mick?"

He laughed and pulled me in close.

"I like creating new words," I said. "It gives them the potential to be more than they are, to be something new. You know what I mean?"

"What else do you do for fun?" he said. "Watch paint dry?"

I gave him a playful slap. He caught my hand and held it against his chest. It was awkward in the most awesome way. It was awksome. He smiled and held the joint to my lips. I took a draw and let it out slow.

I slipped a finger inside his button-down shirt. He put out the joint and slid down the bed. I climbed on top of him. He put his hands on my hips and we kissed. I peeled off my shirt. He said my full-coverage forties bra was the height of sexiness. I peeled that off too. Soon we were naked. Every part of me pressed into every part of him.

I was no longer a puddle. I was vapor. I was lighter than air.

We dozed until the bistro below filled with live music. It was ten p.m. I had a headache.

"We can stay the night," said Buck. "Isaac won't mind."

"I'd better get home."

I was just as naked as I had been hours before but suddenly felt more so. I pulled my clothes under the covers and tried to wriggle into them.

Buck laughed. "You're funny, Poppy."

He leaned over and kissed my back.

I said, "You used a condom, right?"

He said, "You don't remember?"

He'd been fiddling with something, but it felt rude to look and besides that I was too busy thinking, *Oh my God, I'm about to have sex.*

"It was a bit of a blur."

He reached out. "Of course I did. You can always trust me."

I sat up. I wished he wasn't watching me put my bra on. Normally I'd snap it up in front and spin it around but that felt unsophisticated now. I put it on frontwards and reached my hands behind, hoping to hook it together in one seamless movement. On the third attempt Buck did it for me.

"Thanks."

He held me by the shoulders and turned me toward him.

"Come here, darlin'."

I laid my head on his shoulder.

"Was it tender enough?" he whispered.

My heart melted. "Yes."

"You sure?"

I tilted my head and kissed his chin. "I'm sure."

⟿

I woke up early the next morning. It was weird how badly I wanted Cam to know. I imagined saying, *Hey, Cam, guess what I lost?* and he'd say, *Your keys?* and I'd say, *No, my virginity.*

I poured him a bowl of Cheerios and practiced as I walked up the stairs.

Hey, Cam. Guess what I lost?

Good morning, Cameron. Guess what I lost?

Yo. Dude. Guess what I lost?

He opened his door.

"Guess what I found?"

He shrugged. "I dunno. God?"

"That's a weird guess," I said. "How could I lose God?"

"You didn't say *lose*. You said *found*."

"I did?"

"Yep."

"Shit."

"Well," he said, taking the cereal bowl. "Goodbye."

I stuck my foot in the door.

"Wait. Do I look different?"

He looked me up and down. "Maybe slightly more deranged than usual."

I straightened up in an attempt to look sophisticated. "Deranged as in more mature?"

He rolled his eyes. "No. Deranged as in psycho. Can I go back to bed now?"

"Speaking of bed . . ."

"Poppy, did you want something?"

"I shagged the Englishman."

His eyes widened. "You *what*?"

I grinned. "Shagged. You know, as in had sex?"

He pulled me into his room. "But he called you the Pillsbury Doughboy."

"He apologized."

"And you had sex with him?"

I nodded. "Yep."

His jaw dropped. "Oh my God."

"Yeah," I said. "I know."

He cast his Cheerios aside and sat me down beside him. "He used a condom, right?"

"Yes."

"You didn't do it under that disgusting bridge, did you?"

"No."

He looked me up and down again. "It was okay, though, right? I mean, you liked it and everything?"

I smiled. "Afterwards he asked if it was tender enough."

Cam's heart melted too. I could tell.

"I wanted to tell you," I said. "I don't know why."

He looked me up and down for the third time that morning.

"You know how you asked if you looked different?"

"Yeah."

"You do. You look happier."

He reached up, wiped his eyes.

"Are you crying?"

"It's just—I've been waiting so long."

"Waiting?" I said. "For what?"

He wrapped his pinkie around mine. "For you to come back."

That afternoon I went to the bridge. I didn't realize until I was standing there how much I'd missed being below. Now that things were good again with Buck, it was where I wanted to be.

But then there was Thumper.

There was good and bad in everyone but in some people there was just plain evil.

I crept down the embankment. I wanted to know how I'd feel seeing him at a distance.

He wasn't there.

I sat on his folded blankets.

Miracle's sleeping bag was nearby, tied up in bright-purple string.

I wondered what he'd have thought of her once—of her less-than-pure-white complexion.

And what about Lewis? What would Thumper have made of him?

The river trickled as it always did, easily and free.

Before I left, I opened the snub tub. I read them all, every last one.

Dear Poppy,
I am saw-ry that I was grumpy at the cafay when I was
counting balls. I was tired cuz it's hard to sleep
under the bridge.
Love Miracle xoxoxoxo

Thumper,
Sorry I told Poppy about your past. I can be a right
twat when I'm on a bender.
Buck

Lewis,
I'm sorry your grandma refuses to use male
pronouns. Focus on the support you have from
your dad. He loves you and so do we.
Peace and love.
Thumper

Poppy,
Sorry for being a drunken arsehole.
Buck

Poppy,
Sorry that Buck's an ass.
Lewis

I took out a piece of paper and the tiny pencil they kept in the tub. I thought of Cam and wrote, *Hedgehogs, eh? Why can't they just share the hedge?*

CHAPTER SEVEN

Later that night Buck came to my house. He laid on the charm, telling my parents he was taking me to see a documentary film at the cinema.

"You're British," said Mom.

Buck grinned. "Guilty as charged."

Dad noticed the strap of Buck's camera hanging out of his messenger bag.

"A Nikon, huh?" he said. "Bit of a photographer, are you?"

He started going on about Ansel Adams and Henri Cartier-Bresson and I wondered what had happened to him zipping his lips. I cut the conversation short by saying, "Well, we'd better get going. Pip pip, cheerio."

I tugged Buck down the driveway. "So what movie are we going to?"

He took a joint out of his pocket. "It's called *Happiness under the Bridge*."

I laughed. "Sounds amazing."

Turns out it was more like *Sadness under the Bridge*.

Miracle ran to greet us. "Lewis's dad died."

Buck picked her up, all three feet of her. She wept on his shoulder with Gilbert tight in her grip.

I felt wobbly at the sight in front of me. There was Lewis, his head in Thumper's lap, Thumper's arthritic fingers running through his hair. *Shh-shh-shh.*

I wasn't sure what to do. I knelt beside them. I looked to Thumper for comfort. The look he gave back was a hug.

Miracle joined us. I put my hand on Lewis's back. He looked up. "Oh, Poppy."

He sat up and I held him tight.

"I'm all alone now," he said.

Thumper said, "As long as I live, that will never be true."

Lewis smiled and wiped his eyes. "I have to get back. They're coming to take him soon."

I pictured his dad, dead in Plan 47-11.

"Miracle and I will walk with you," said Buck.

I wondered if Lewis would want Buck around.

"That'd be nice," said Lewis.

Buck nodded to me as they left. Then he nodded at Thumper.

It was an uncomfortable silence at first. But then I linked my arm around his.

He cleared his throat. "I guess you haven't goggled me yet."

"It's *google*," I said. "And yes, I did."

He stared straight ahead. "And here you sit with your arm around mine."

I pictured his knobby fingers running through Lewis's hair.

"You know that battle you were talking about?" I said. "The one that runs through the heart of every man?"

His eyes searched mine. "Yes?"

"The war is over now, Thumper. You've won."

His voice cracked. "You think so?"

I nodded at his bible. "I know so."

He picked it up, held it close to his chest.

"I wrote it while I was in prison."

The wobble I had felt earlier was back. "You were in prison?"

"Ten years."

"I'm sorry."

"Don't be. It changed my life."

"How?"

"I found the meaning of it."

"Life?" I said.

He nodded.

"Care to share it?"

"That," he said, with a sparkle in his eyes, "you have to find out for yourself."

⤙

I went home early.

Cam was on the couch. I sat beside him.

"You okay, Popsicle? You seem jittery."

I wrapped my arms around his waist. "My friend's dad died."

I buried my head in his chest. I would have burrowed into him if I could.

He held me tight.

Shh–shh–shh.

⤙

I woke up in the morning drained and thinking of Lewis. I wondered how he'd slept, if he'd spent the night alone.

I went online and watched a video of a dying man. It made me feel better, as if I'd somehow shared Lewis's pain.

Cam poked his head in my door. "You're watching happy things, right?"

I nodded. "Yes."

I made my answer truthful by putting on one of my favorite movies—*White Christmas*. Bing Crosby and Danny Kaye were entertaining the troops somewhere in Europe. The soldiers looked sad during Bing's melancholic rendition of "White Christmas," but I figured missing Christmas makes future ones even more special and besides, the war would be over by 1945.

I could almost feel Lewis's shoulder bumping gently into mine. He'd say something like, *Miracle's dad died in Afghanistan, you know. War is nothing to be nostalgic about.* That's what I figured he'd say anyway. It was because we had a connection now. That's what it was all about.

I closed my eyes and imagined that the tree was up, the turkey was in the oven, and there was snow falling outside.

Then I imagined Cam in a battlefield far away from home.

I opened my eyes and re-watched the opening scene.

This time, I cried.

✐

Lewis came for a walk just as the movie ended.

We didn't talk. We didn't have to. We'd talk when we were ready.

I followed Lewis off the tracks. I didn't know where we were going. It didn't matter.

We ended up at Regent Park and sat side by side on the swings.

I spoke first. "How are you?"

He reached into his pocket.

"He wrote it himself."

He passed me a piece of lined paper. "Read the high-lighted bit."

I cleared my throat. "'Lewis Liu leaves to mourn his son, Lewis Jr., of whom he was incredibly proud.'"

I smiled.

"He switched from *her* to *him* the day I told him," he said. "I was lucky to have him."

I folded the paper and passed it back. "And he was lucky to have you."

"My future is up in the air now," he said. "How will I get through it without my dad?"

He tilted his head back, his eyes focused on the sky.

"It's okay," I said. "You can cry."

He let his head fall. His tears too.

I put my hand on the back of his head, ran my fingers across his shaved bits. It felt nice.

There was no awkwardness with Lewis, no wondering what he'd say or do next. It was like I'd known him forever. Soon he'd stop crying and I'd say, *You okay now?* and he'd say, *Yeah, thanks*, and then we'd sit in silence and it would be comfortable. Being with Lewis was wonderfully pre-dictable—it was Honeycombs for breakfast and the way Cam signed off his texts with six *x*'s and six *o*'s.

Lewis wiped his eyes. "My grandmother has come to stay. She doesn't like me very much. She's selling the house. She says I'll have to move in with her on the other side of town."

My heart sunk. "Is there no one else?"

"There's an aunt. But she's in Vancouver."

I took his hand. "Oh, Lewis."

He ran his thumb across my knuckles. "I read everything in the snub tub today. The hedgehog joke made me laugh."

"My brother told me that one," I said. "He's my antidote to sadness."

"He is?"

I nodded. "Velcro—what a rip-off."

He laughed, so I told him another.

"It's hard to explain puns to kleptomaniacs—they always take things so literally."

"Poppy?" he said.

"Yeah?"

"Will you be *my* antidote to sadness?"

"I would," I said. "But I don't think I'm potent enough."

He looked at me in a way that felt thoughtful and deep. "Let's head back."

After a bit he said, "So. You forgave Buck."

"He has a softer side. He just doesn't show it."

"A few weeks ago you wanted to cross the road and punch him in the face."

"Nah. I only cross the road when I'm being chased by Colonel Sanders."

He smiled. "You're wrong, Poppy. You *are* strong enough. You're extra-strength."

"Like Viagra," I said.

"Sure," he said, grinning. "Like Viagra."

Lewis ran into a corner store. When he came out he said, "I bet Buck has never bought you a Popsicle."

I broke it in half. "You really don't like him, do you?"

He answered quickly. "Nope."

I passed him his half of the Popsicle. When our fingers touched he looked away.

⁓

I went to work to find flames licking out of the oven and Mr. Chen squinting at the instructions on the fire extinguisher. I snatched it from him and squeezed the handle. Foam sprayed everywhere, dousing the flames.

I leaned against the counter and caught my breath. "Jesus Christ."

Mr. Chen reached into the oven and pulled out a rubber chicken.

I reached into the broom closet and pulled out Miracle. "Apologize to Mr. Chen," I said.

She bowed her head as if she was praying and then she looked up. "Soz."

I gave her a warning look. "Not funny. Say it properly."

Mr. Chen snapped. "You could have burned the whole shop down, Merry-girl!"

The harshness of his voice sent Miracle's bottom lip trembling. She bolted.

Mr. Chen looked me up and down. "Don't just stand there like a lump," he said. "Go after her!"

She was gone from my sight within minutes.

I ran around Elgin like a chicken with its head cut off. I couldn't find her anywhere.

I sat on the curb with my head in my hands.

A moment later, a voice. "Do you need an ambulance?"

"No," I said. "I don't need an ambulance."

She crouched in front of me.

"Are you dying? It sounds like you're dying."

"Just . . . give me a second, okay?"

She sat beside me. "Mr. Chen hates me."

"No, he doesn't."

"If I get taken away he won't even miss me."

"You won't get taken away."

"How do you know?"

"Because Buck said so."

She moved from the curb and straddled my lap, her head against my chest. Her double buns tickled my nose. I put my hands on her back, felt the rise and fall of her breath. I thought about breathing—the in and the out that keeps us alive all day long—through the good and the bad. That was what we were meant to do, I supposed. Survive.

Cam was shaving his chest when I got home. I sat on the edge of the tub.

"Why are you using my shaving cream?"

"Because mine smells like a lumberjack."

"What do lumberjacks smell like?"

"Pine needles, apple cider, and the great outdoors."

I laughed. "Going out with the Drome-drearies tonight?"

"No. I'm going to work."

"Tonight? Won't the shop be closed?"

"Fabe's having a cocktail party for VIP customers."

Saying *awesome* would come across as insincere so I said, "That's nice."

He finished shaving his chest and moved to his face.

"Guess what, Pops?"

"What?"

"If I could rearrange the alphabet I'd put *u* and *i* together."

My sweet Cam.

I smiled. "Speaking of letters . . ."

146

He raised an eyebrow. "Yes?"

"You know the *T* in *LGBT*?"

"Yeah . . ."

"If you're a boy who likes girls but you were born a girl, does that make you a lesbian even though in your head and your heart you're one hundred percent boy?"

He looked back at his own reflection and continued shaving. "I think you just answered your own question. A transgender boy is one hundred percent boy and therefore is like anyone else—they're either straight, into girls—or gay, into guys. Or they can fall anywhere in between . . . just like anyone else."

"That's what I thought. It gets confusing sometimes."

"It's only confusing when people focus on the gender a person is at birth, instead of the gender they identify with. Which really sucks for transgender people when they want to pee."

I frowned. "People care where transgender people pee?"

"People lose their shit about it all the time. They think transgender females are wolves in sheep's clothing and the only reason they want to use the women's bathroom is so that they can attack 'real' women. Not because, you know, they might just need the toilet."

I sighed. "Cam? What's the point?"

"The point of what?"

"Everything."

He went back to the mirror. "I guess the point is to try to be happy, and when someone stops you from doing it you fight like hell until you win."

"What kind of life is that?" I asked.

"One that can change the world. Think about it, Pops. I can get married to another man now. Legally. That wasn't always the case. But people fought for the right and I, for one, am thankful they didn't throw their hands up and say, *What's the point?*"

I stood up and wrapped my arms around his waist. "I am too."

I went downstairs to find Mom and Dad watching the news. For some reason, I longed to sit between them. I went to the coffee table and picked up a magazine. I looked at the space where Mom ended and Dad began. I'd have fitted there once. Dad caught my eye. He inched to the left, invited me with a nod.

Our legs were touching. I wondered if they felt the tingling. I looked at my dad's hand, remembered how it used to feel wrapped around mine, big and rough and warm.

Cam was leaving for Bliss when prime minister Justin Trudeau appeared on the screen. Mom nodded toward the TV. "Watch."

We are sorry ...
For stripping you of your dignity;
For robbing you of your potential;
For treating you like you were dangerous, indecent,
    and flawed;

...

It is our collective shame that you were so mistreated.
    And it is our collective shame that this apology
    took so long—many who suffered are no longer
    alive to hear these words. And for that, we are
    truly sorry.

Mom cried. So did Cam.

Dad reached for my hand. It was just as I remembered.

———※———

Later that night, Buck stood on the doorstep with his elbow out. "Would madam like an escort?"

"An escort?" I said. "Working as a prostitute now, are you?"

He linked my arm through his. "I prefer the term *gigolo.*"

Mom and Dad watched approvingly from the window. Buck gave them a wave. I laughed. "You've got them fooled."

He shrugged. "What can I say? I'm the master of deception."

We walked down the train tracks. I told him about the royal train. He said he didn't give a toss about the monarchy, that they were as useless as a chocolate teapot. I laughed and said, "You have a royal look about you. You could be Prince Harry's younger brother." He asked if that was good. I said, "Yes. Harry is as fit as a butcher's dog."

"The royal butcher's dog," he said.

"Yes," I said. "Even better."

The river under the bridge was louder than usual, but in a good way, and the air had a marshmallow smell. Lewis and Miracle sat by a fire with sticky-sweet smiles. Thumper lay curled up nearby.

"It's his arthritis," said Lewis.

Buck lit a joint and put it to Thumper's lips. "You'll be right as rain soon, mate."

Thumper must have been in agony to inhale so deeply.

Lewis moved him closer to us. He told us stories and after a while he looked less pained. He said he lived in a caravan once, on a berry farm in the South of England. He said that the berry pickers were from Romania. He said that the locals looked down on them, because they were immigrants, but they were good people, as good as gold. He said they taught him some Romanian.

"*A băga mâna în foc pentru cineva.*"

"What does that mean?" I asked.

"It means that you'd put your hand in fire for somebody."

"Why would someone want to do that?" asked Miracle.

"It means you'd vouch for them, that you believe in them," he said.

He had a faraway look on his face and we lost ourselves in it, imagining ourselves on a berry farm in the South of England.

He said, "I'd have put my hand in the fire for any of those people."

That was when Cam appeared.

"Who's that?" asked Miracle.

"That's my brother," I said. But I barely recognized him. I wanted him to stomp across the concrete like a runway model on crack but he just stood there, hunched over with his hands in his pockets.

He looked up. There was blood on his lip.

I went to him. "What happened?"

His voice was a whisper.

"He didn't ask if it was tender enough."

I wasn't sure what to do, where to go, who to call. I just stood there frozen.

Lewis brought Cam to the fire. Thumper put a cloth to his lip. "You're safe here." My eyes welled up.

Miracle climbed into Cam's lap. I reached for her but Cam wrapped his arms around her. He put his nose in her hair and closed his eyes.

Buck crouched next to him. "What happened, mate?"

He said it calmly. "My boss assaulted me."

I knew what that meant.

Lewis put his arm around me.

"We should call the police," said Thumper.

"Don't bother," said Miracle. "Mama says they don't care."

She closed her eyes and popped her thumb in her mouth.

My heart broke into a million pieces.

We walked home, the two of us, in silence. I made small talk with Mom and Dad while Cam slipped upstairs. When I went to my room he was in my bed. We snuggled together, like we were safe and sound in our mother's womb.

"Tell me what happened, Cam."

He rolled away from me. I thought it was because he didn't want to talk. But he did.

"He asked me to stay after the VIP party, to help tidy up. He came up behind me, started massaging my shoulders. I tried to shrug him off but he told me he just wanted to say thanks, for staying late."

I put my hand on his shoulder, wondered where else Fabe's hands had gone.

"I let him massage me, but I hated it. I didn't know what else to do. He's my boss."

"Oh, Cam."

"He kept telling me to relax. I couldn't. I was tense. He was getting mad, I could hear it in his voice. I could feel his breath on my neck, then his lips. I swung around, told him to back off. That's when he grabbed me, pulled me into the back room. He said I was ungrateful, that he'd given me a job when I had no experience."

My blood began to boil.

"He was all over me, Pops. I couldn't think straight. His hand, his mouth . . . they were everywhere. He was so . . . rough."

Tears pricked my eyes. I struggled to find the words. When I finally did they were all wrong.

"All those boxing lessons," I said. "Why didn't you fight?"

Cam spun round. Raw anger flashed in his eyes. "Are you serious right now?"

"It's just that you're trained to fight . . ."

"Would it have been my fault if I hadn't?"

"That's not what I meant."

He glared at me before turning to face the ceiling.

I reached out, touched his arm. "Are you mad at me?"

He laughed. "It's not always about you, Pops."

I reached for his pinkie. He pulled it away.

I was hurt and he was angry but I needed to know.

"Cam?" I asked. "How far did it go?"

He rolled over and faced the wall. "Far enough."

The next morning I went to Lewis's house. His grand-mother answered the door.

"Is Lewis here?"

She looked me up and down. "She's busy," she said. "She can't come out right now."

For a second I thought I had the wrong house.

"Too bad," I said. "I was hoping *he* could come for a walk."

A moment later, Lewis brushed past her.

"Come on, Poppy. Let's go."

We headed toward Regent Park.

"She's horrible," I said.

"Yes," he said. "She is."

He didn't ask about Cam and I was glad. There was so

much I wanted to say, but the thoughts in my head were like a tangle of wires and when I tried to separate them electric shocks would shoot across my brain.

We sat side by side on the swings in silence.

After a while, Lewis swung sideways and bumped my shoulder with his.

And just like that, my thoughts began to unravel.

"Lewis?"

"Yeah?"

"Have you ever wished that spoken words were like words on paper? That once they came out of your mouth you could reach out, give them a brush with some Wite-Out, and make them disappear forever?"

"Uh-oh," he said. "What did you say?"

I stared at the gravel under my feet.

"I asked Cam why he didn't fight back."

Lewis cringed. "Yikes."

"I feel terrible. Why would I say something like that?"

"It makes the world seem less scary if the victim's partly to blame."

I looked at him sharply. "I don't blame Cam for what happened."

"Then why did you ask him that question?"

I felt my face turn red—with anger, embarrassment, shame.

"I—"

My wires were getting tangled again and tears stung my eyes.

"Why don't you give me a break, Lewis? I feel guilty enough as it is."

"I'm just making a point," he said. "There's a whole psychology around victim blaming. People want to believe the world is good, that good things happen to good people and bad things happen to bad people. When bad things happen to good people, it feels as though no one is safe, so they rationalize it to feel less vulnerable."

"You're making me sound really selfish. My brother was assaulted and my heart is broken! And trust me, I know that bad things happen to good people. I watched a cat get put in a microwave and I am sure that cat was a pretty good person!"

I was shaking from head to toe.

He stood up. "Take a breath, Poppy."

"Take a breath? Why don't I just hold it if I'm such a rotten person? Why don't I hold it until I pass out? That way you would disappear because you are a horrible little know-it-all!"

The way his face fell, it crushed my heart a little. I was about to say sorry but he spoke first.

"I didn't mean to sound like a know-it-all. Everything I said, I'd read it in a doctor's waiting room, in *Psychology Today*. It was really interesting so I remembered it. I thought that telling you about it might help—because then you'd know that your reaction is not unusual—but now you feel even worse and I feel like an arrogant jerk."

He crouched in front of me, put his hands on my knees. "I'm sorry for upsetting you."

I took his hands. "It's okay," I said.

He ran his thumb across my knuckles. "I don't get it," I said. "If he was looking for sex, why didn't he go for someone his own age?"

"It wasn't about sex," said Lewis. "It was about power."

I pictured it in my head, Fabian overpowering Cam, hurting him, trying to have his way with him. It sounded like he almost did.

Lewis took my hands, pulled me to standing.

"Come here, Poppy."

He wrapped his arms around me. I laid my head on his chest. "You're a good friend, Lewis."

I felt his shoulders slump slightly. "You are too."

I straightened up and wiped my eyes.

"Poppy," Lewis said, "do you think you can spare a few minutes?"

"Sure," I said. "Why?"

"The cemetery is not far. It would be nice to have company."

I pointed at a nearby corner shop. "We could bring flowers."

Lewis let me pick. I chose daisies. He said they were perfect.

As we walked through the graveyard I felt thankful to have two living parents and wondered how Lewis would cope with being alone.

He stopped at his mother's headstone. He said, "Don't worry, Mom. Dad will be here soon." When he bent to lay the flowers his shirtsleeve moved up, revealing not one armband tattoo but two.

It was all too much.

Everything was too much.

I stepped forward and put a hand behind his back. "Are you okay?"

"Yes," he said. "I'm okay."

On the way back, he said, "Poppy? Why did you come to me today and not Buck?"

The wires in my mind were tangle-free but I struggled to find an answer.

"You were closer."

The rest of the way home I wondered if what I'd just said was true.

⇀

As soon as I got home I checked on him.

"You okay, Cam?"

He was sitting on his bed, staring into space.

"I wanted to say sorry."

"For what?" he said. "Implying I was too gay to fight back?"

"I never said that."

"You called me one-dimensional once. I know what that meant. It was code—for too over-the-top, too flamboyant."

"That's not what I meant at all," I said. "I'm really sorry if it came across that way."

"Just go, Pops. I've been up all night with my own guilt. I don't need yours too."

"Guilt?" I said. "Guilt about what?"

Cam shrugged. "Maybe I sent him some kind of signal, without even knowing it."

"What happened wasn't about sex," I said. "It was about power."

Cam snorted. "Oooh. Listen to you. One minute you're an ignorant victim blamer and the next you're an enlightened advocate."

I sighed. "I never said it was your fault, Cam."

"Whatever, Pops."

"Don't be mad at me, Cam. Please."

He picked up his phone, stared at the screen.

I wanted to go to him, put my arms around him, and tell him everything would be okay.

"If you want I can help you break the news to Mom or Dad," I said. "Just let me know."

He looked up. "Are you kidding me? I'm not telling anyone about this. Ever. And neither are you. Got it?"

The edge on his voice cut me to the core.

"Cam—"

"Promise me, Poppy."

I'd have done anything to soften that edge. "I promise."

I looked at him, up and down and all around. "Just so you know," I said, "I don't think you're *too* anything. All I've ever wanted is for you to be yourself."

He fixed his eyes back on his phone. "You can go now."

My sweet Cam. He was no longer the antidote to sadness—he was the poster boy.

I walked up and down Elgin feeling not like a chicken but like something less.

A life form at its lowest level.

An organism. No. A microbe.

Microbes caused disease.

Mr. Chen shouted at me from the shop door. "More oomph, Poppy Flower, more oomph!"

Miracle tugged on his shirt. When he bent down she whispered in his ear. A moment later he waved me over.

He looked me up and down. "You always did strike me as a dimwit. Why didn't you tell me about your brother?"

I glanced at Miracle. "What did she tell you?"

I was scared for her, for what she might have understood from the other night.

He answered as if it were a trick question. "She said your brother was beat up."

"Yes, that's right," I said. "He was."

"Well, go home," he said. "Be with him."

"I think I'd rather work," I said. "But thanks anyway."

He gave me a questioning look. "Are you sure?"

I nodded.

He shrugged. "Well, feel free to spend your shift on the barbershop bench. You do most of the time anyway."

Miracle sat beside me. Her feet couldn't reach the ground so she kicked her shoes together to make the soles light up.

"Poppy?"

"Yes?"

"Do you want to be a chicken when you grow up?"

"Pfssh. No."

"What do you want to be, then?"

I took the opportunity to try to inspire her. "I want to be like Rosie the Riveter."

"Does she live on James Street?"

I laughed. "No. She's not a real person. She's a—"

"Clown?"

"No."

"Elephant?"

"No. She's more of a symbol . . . an icon."

"Like the poop emoji?"

Inspiring six-year-olds was hard.

"Basically," I said, "when I grow up I want to do something badass."

Miracle hopped up and did a backflip.

"Like that?"

"Jesus, Miracle. You're going to give me a heart attack."

"Have you been practicing?" she asked.

"Backflips? No."

"That's the only way you'll get better. I started on a trampoline. Now I can do it on concrete."

"Hence the heart attack," I said.

She sat back down.

"Do you know what my mother grew up to be?"

One way or another, she was going to kill me.

"I'm . . . not sure?"

"She gives massages in her bedroom."

"Oh. That's . . . interesting."

"She doesn't have a license though. If you don't have a license a social worker comes and takes your kids."

I didn't know what to say so I put my arm around her and pulled her in close.

"Is giving massages badass?" she asked.

"Um, yeah, sure. I mean, it's hard work, kneading on people's backs and stuff."

"Lewis babysits me when Mama works because having a kid around is not very per-fessional."

"Yes," I said. "I can see that."

"Poppy?"

"Yeah?"

"I'm going to be famous someday."

It took everything in me to keep from saying, *No. You won't.*

She hopped up from the bench and took a piece of chalk out of her pocket. She drew a circle on the sidewalk and labeled it *Miracle's stage*. She stood in the center and sang about being touched for the very first time. Six years old and singing Madonna's "Like a Virgin." I actually clutched my feathery heart. I wanted to change her stage to a globe. I'd draw a stick girl underneath, holding it up with two strong arms. I'd say, *Look, Miracle. That's you. You can have it all.* At least until the next time it rained.

I went back to the shop.

"Mr. Chen?"

He looked up from the deep-fat fryer. "Yes?"

"You said I could go home. I still don't want to but there's somewhere else I need to be. And I want to take Miracle."

Miracle looked confused but Mr. Chen didn't hesitate. "Do whatever it is you have to do, Poppy Flower."

⚜

As we approached the arena Miracle said, "I came here on a field trip. I didn't fall once. The teacher said I was unnatural."

"I think you mean *a natural*," I said. "That means you're really good at something."

I put my hand on the door handle. My heart started to beat double time.

"Although, if you think about it, *unnatural* would work too. I mean, it's natural for little kids to fall when they're new to skating, so not falling could be considered pretty unnatural, I guess."

Miracle squinted through the glass. "Are we going in or what?"

I could see Eddie behind the front desk. He waved us in. "Here to watch the game?"

I felt a tingle of excitement. "There's a game today?"

He looked at the clock. "Right after practice."

I squeezed Miracle's hand. "You're in luck."

⚜

Eve shrieked when she saw me. "Poppy!"

Within seconds I was surrounded in a group hug.

"Ouch," said Eve. "Jesus Christ."

It was Miracle, forcing her way through the huddle.

Eve rubbed her hip. "Someone get this girl a pair of skates. She'd make an awesome jammer."

The girls were in full bout makeup—Wanda Onda Warpath had painted a Ziggy Stardust–inspired lightning bolt across her eye, and Katniss Evermean had transformed her face into a sugar skull. Miracle looked at them in awe.

Eve said, "You guys here to watch the game?"

I grinned. "We are now."

They did all the usual drills—starts and stops, one-foot glides, double-knee falls. I stole a sideways glance at Miracle. She was entranced.

I leaned in. "So? What do you think?"

She pointed at Bashin' Robbins's legs. "I want tights with holes all over them, just like hers."

I tried not to let my disapproval show.

A few minutes later, Eve appeared with Miracle-sized skates.

"Hey, kid," she said. "Want to give it a go?"

Miracle nodded. "Can I have makeup too?"

While the new girl, Miss Fortune, painted rainbows on her cheeks, Miracle reached out and stroked Eve's hot-pink satin hot pants. "I like your underwear."

I thrust a mouthguard into Miracle's mouth. "They're not underwear," I said. "They're shorts."

The safety gear made Miracle look tiny. I hoped she'd be okay.

Eve took her onto the rink. Miracle skated once around the track, then popped her mouthguard out. "Look, Poppy! I'm unnatural."

I watched like a proud mama.

Eve gave Miracle the helmet cover with the star designation. "You're the jammer now," she said. "You have to bust through the pack. Just like you did with the group hug."

They began skating around the track, the pack at the front, Miracle at the back. The blockers left plenty of gaps, which Miracle skated through low and fast. When she made it to the other side she pumped her arms like a bodybuilder.

She was the VIP of everything.

When the Iron Maidens arrived, Miracle and I found a spot on the bleachers. We stayed for the whole bout.

Halfway through the game, Miracle said she wanted muscles like Intoxiskate. My heart swelled.

When the Brawlipops won, Miracle said it was the best day of her life and I thought, *Wow, it doesn't take much.*

CHAPTER EIGHT

A week went by. Cam wouldn't talk. My loudmouthed, confident brother . . . mute. He told our parents he had the flu. They believed him. Every time I went to his room he pretended to sleep. I said, "You have to talk to me sometime."

I wanted to help him, to be his support. But he wanted nothing to do with me.

I guess I was his bad outweighing the good.

Maybe it was time to tip the scales.

⇒

I spent twenty minutes warming up, swinging my arm, rehearsing my line. I'd never given anyone a knuckle sandwich before.

I could see him through the window, adding the finishing touches to a client's hair.

When the last customer left the shop I walked in like I owned the place.

Fabian came toward me. He had a black eye, a swollen nose, and some scrapes on the bottom of his chin.

Cam *had* fought back.

"Sorry, we're closed."

I'd had it all planned. I was going to ask if he was hungry. And if he said yes—and surely he would have as it was the end of his shift—I was going to say, *Here, have a knuckle sandwich.*

But a knuckle sandwich seemed lame now—now that Cam had given him a three-course meal.

"Can I help you?" he said.

I looked at his hands. I wanted to break his fingers.

He had a turned-up nose. He was a pig. A nasty, horrible, deviant pig. And pigs loved to eat.

"I was just wondering," I said. "Are you hungry?"

He looked into my eyes. "Are you on something?"

I made a fist.

"You're not planning on hitting me, are you?"

He had a smirk on his face that needed wiping off. I pulled my arm back and punched him across the chin.

"That was for my brother."

I took off running. I couldn't wait to get home. Cam would see me sweaty and shaking and out of breath and he'd know—I would do anything for him. We could even do away with the pinkie promises because my word was so solid it didn't need gimmicks.

I crept into the house and snuck up the stairs. He was sitting at his vanity, staring into the mirror.

"Guess what?"

"What?"

I showed him my knuckles. He stared at them blankly.

"I punched the bastard," I said. "I went to Bliss and I punched him. Right in the face."

He looked back at the mirror.

"Did you hear me?" I said.

"Yeah. I heard you."

"And?"

He picked up one of his lipsticks and dropped it in the trash. "You think one little punch makes everything better?"

"No, I just thought—"

He threw in his mascara too. "He didn't steal my granola bar, Pops."

I moved the trash can away from him. "Why are you throwing your makeup away?"

"Because I don't feel like myself anymore."

"Maybe we can put it in a box," I said. "Until you're ready to wear it again."

He rolled his eyes. "I don't need your meaningless advice, Poppy."

I sat on the edge of his bed, wished I could reach out and touch him. I wished I had a magic wand that would make everything better.

I traced my finger along the striped pattern of his bed-spread. "I saw Fabian's face," I said. "Looks like you gave him a good beating."

"Good thing," he said. "Otherwise someone might think I just let it happen."

I sighed. "I said I was sorry. Can't we just move on?"

He stared at his reflection in the mirror.

"It's like being inside a big block of ice," he said. "You just stand there, frozen in fear, wishing you could escape, but you can't."

My poor Cam.

I looked at my knuckles. "I just wanted you to know . . . I'd do anything for you."

He looked up. "Can you turn back time?"

"No—"

"Then you're basically useless."

"Cam—"

"I'm going to bed now, Poppy."

I looked at his alarm clock. "It's not even nine o'clock."

He turned to face me. "I know how to tell time."

His face was like stone. He stared at me till I shut the door.

I went to the living room. I started with "I have some-thing to tell you" and ended with "Maybe you should call the police." I used the word *assault* and let them fill in the blanks. I broke my parents' hearts and stole their souls. Dad pulled me tight to his chest. He smelled like I remembered, like the air in the kitchen at Christmas, all cinnamon-y and good.

I asked if I could stay the night with friends. They said yes. Then they looked at each other with eyes that were lost and headed up to see Cam.

I went straight to the bridge. They were all there.

"I told my parents about Cam."

"How'd they take it?" asked Lewis.

"They're devastated."

Buck rubbed my back. "Well, it probably didn't come as a complete shocker."

I twisted away from him. "What's that supposed to mean?"

"Well," he said, "it's a well-known fact that gay men are way more promiscuous than straight guys."

There was a stunned silence.

I stood up. "Screw you, Buck."

He chased me up the embankment. "Poppy, stop."

I turned to face him. "Can we ever spend time together without you saying something stupid?"

"What did I say?"

"First of all, Cam is not a man, he's a boy. And he was assaulted. And second of all, your 'well-known fact,' as you call it, is a load of crap."

"I'm sorry, Pidge."

"You're always sorry."

"I say things I don't mean. I don't know why."

"I don't either. All I know is I'm sick of it."

"What can I do to make it better?"

"Take a vow of silence?"

He zipped his lips. I didn't laugh.

He opened his arms. I walked into them because I was too tired to fight and, what's more, I just didn't care anymore. If bad overpowered good then so be it.

Maybe that's all I deserved anyway.

"I still have the key to Isaac's," he said.

I took his hand. "Let's go."

He kept the conversation light. He listed all the chocolate bars he missed from back home—Wispas, Yorkies, Curly Wurlys, Flakes. I asked him if he ate fish and chips every night and he said yes, at the top of Big Ben. When we got to the apartment he tucked me into bed. He ran downstairs to the bistro and brought back hot chocolate and donuts. *Lady and the Tramp* appeared on the flat-screen

TV. We sang the Siamese-cat song even though it felt racist, and then he said, "Good night, Pidge" and turned out the light. He was ninety percent asshole and ten percent hero. He was chocolate during a diet. He was like a last meal on death row—indulgent, delicious, irrelevant.

I wrapped my arms around his waist. "Tell me it'll be okay."

He was the king of bullshit.

"It'll be okay, love."

I closed my eyes. My dreams were of Cam.

When I got home the next morning there was a police cruiser outside. I stood in the hallway and listened. Miracle was wrong. The cops *did* care. They told Cam he was brave and that he wasn't alone. They said he had nothing to feel ashamed about, that it wasn't his fault.

When the cops left I went to his room. "I know that was hard," I said, "but this is good, right? Fabian will get arrested. And you'll get support."

He looked up. "*This is good.*" He said it two, three, four times, as if he were rehearsing a line for a play, ingraining it in his memory. He started laughing. He was wearing grey track pants and a hoodie, like he was some kind of prisoner. He was almost unrecognizable. I read once that happy tears and sad tears looked different under a microscope. Cam might have been laughing, but I figured what was running down his face had the molecular structure of sadness.

He wiped his eyes. "Thanks, Poppy. That was hysterical. I can always count on you for a laugh."

I was still in the doorway. I moved closer, even though I was scared. Of him. Of the way he was staring at me. Of the way he was squeezing the four fingers of his right hand with the four fingers of his left. *Be careful with that pinkie*, I thought. *That pinkie is mine.*

I stood at the end of his bed. "I was just trying to help."

"You made things worse."

"It felt like the right thing to do."

"Funny," he said. "Telling Mom and Dad about the photo felt like the right thing to do too. But I didn't. You know why? Because you asked me not to!"

"This is worse."

His face softened. "Is it? You've been pretty messed up, Poppy. And I've been pretty worried."

"You've been worried?"

He pointed at the door. "Get out, Poppy."

"Don't be mad."

He stood up and opened the door. "Go."

The air was being sucked out of me. Because I couldn't breathe, the tears came without sound.

"Here we go," he said. "Cue the waterworks."

He had a beautiful face, even when he was hurt and angry and sad. I wanted to touch it. I wanted all of his Cam-ness to transfer from his body into my fingers and through my whole being.

I managed a whisper. "I'm sorry."

"You can say sorry all you want," he said. "I had to tell my parents what happened in that back room. I had to give the details to the cops. Do you know how hard that was? I will never, ever forgive you."

※

My parents, not ours. I was no longer part of them, part of him. Still, I could feel him, the way amputees could feel pain in their missing limbs. He was my phantom brother. And all I wanted was to be part of him again.

※

I tried on all my outfits. I watched the Andrews Sisters sing about apple trees and I played the air bugle.

And I still felt like shit.

※

I went to the end of my street, sat on a neighbor's brick wall. A police cruiser pulled up to the house. The officer knocked but nobody answered. I waved him down as he drove past. He stopped, got out of the car.

"Everything okay?"

I shook my head no.

He sat on the wall with me. "What's up?"

"I killed my brother," I said.

He didn't believe me. I couldn't see why. Anyone could murder anyone. It happened all the time. It wasn't just weird, creepy people—it could be the little old lady next door. She could smack someone over the head with a frying pan because they refused her a cup of sugar.

"You killed your brother?" he said. "Really?"

He looked strong. Probably never ate a donut in his life.

"I killed him figuratively," I said. "I crushed his soul. He'll never be the same again."

He smiled and I said, "It's not funny."

"Of course it's not," he said.

His accent made me think of palm trees. I said, "Do you like Bob Marley?" and wondered if that was racist.

"Of course," he said. Then he sang, "'Don't worry, about a thing.'" He said *thing* without the *h*.

"You live around here?" he asked.

My eyes flicked to my house. "No."

A call came in on his radio. He went to his car and answered it. I wondered what I'd have to do for him to arrest me. I wanted to get locked up in a dirty, stinky jail cell with a toilet right there in the middle of it that I'd have to use with the guards watching. That'd teach me for being a snitch.

When he came back I said, "I smoke marijuana."

He sat next to me. "You didn't crush your brother's soul. You saved it."

I blinked back tears. "He said I made things worse by telling."

"You made it better. He'll get the help he needs now."

I nodded toward the house. "They're home, you know. They just didn't answer."

"That's okay. I'll come back."

Before he got in his car I said, "Did you hear what I said? I did drugs. I smoked marijuana."

"I heard you," he said.

Then he drove away.

⇒

I went home and sat outside Cam's bedroom door. I fell asleep there. When I woke I didn't move. I just stayed on the floor looking under the crack. He came out to go downstairs to the bathroom. I said, "I wish I didn't tell.

I'd take it all back if I could." He stepped over me like I was a piece of dog shit. On his way back he said, "And the Academy Award goes to . . ."

The door missed my nose by an inch.

*

I imagined myself in drought-ridden Africa surrounded by toddlers with sunken eyes. We couldn't cry because our tears were dried up. I kept that image in my mind until the moment passed, then I went to my room and re-watched the video of a cat being put in a microwave.

*

I went to the bridge. I wanted to see Buck. I wanted him to call me Pidge and lie about everything being okay.

He wasn't there.

Miracle's mom brought pizzas. She kissed Miracle on the cheek and told her to have fun.

I whispered to Lewis. "That's messed up."

"What is?" he said.

"She kisses her goodbye like she's dropping her off at a slumber party or something. She acts like everything's normal."

"Actually," he said, "things *are* kind of normal. Tonight

is Miracle's last night here. Her Mom's not working nights anymore."

"She's not?"

"Nope. She offered me a room too. Said I could stay as long as I liked."

"What about your grandmother?" I asked.

He smiled. "She was relieved. It was a win-win."

Something happened inside my chest.

"You okay, Poppy?"

"I think my heart just swelled."

He looked at my chest. "It did?"

I nodded. "Tell me more good things."

Lewis smiled. "My grandmother found a buyer for the house. She said that all the proceeds of the sale go to me. She said it's what my dad wanted."

"You mean . . ."

He nodded. "And my aunt said she'll fly out to be with me when the time comes."

I clutched my chest. "I'm literally the Grinch right now."

He laughed. "Your heart grew three sizes?"

"Or more."

He cast his eyes down to the little wooden boy walking across his wrist. "I'll be a real boy soon."

I touched his face. "You're a real boy now."

Buck rounded the corner just as Lewis laid his hand on mine.

"Get your mitts off my girlfriend."

He was drunk. I could tell by the way he looked at the pizza. It was as if each pie were a magical creature. It took him three attempts to grab a slice. He waved it in Lewis's face. "You're bang out of order, mate. You'd better watch yourself."

Miracle tried to lighten the mood. "Hey, Buck. What do you get when you cross an apple and a Christmas tree?"

The answer was written all over his pizza.

"I don't bloody well know, do I?" He shoved the slice in his mouth, then spit it out. "Fucking hell. Who puts pineapple on pizza?"

I opened my arms to Miracle.

"That was a good joke," said Lewis. "I have one too. Want to hear it?"

She nodded.

"What's a vampire's favorite fruit?"

She shrugged.

"A neck-tarine."

She smiled.

"How about this one?" he said. "How is history like a fruitcake?"

"It's full of crap," said Buck.

"Actually," I said, "it's full of dates."

"Oooh," said Buck. "Get a load of Miss Smarty-pants and her best friend, the freaky HeShe."

Lewis's jaw hardened.

"Ignore him," I whispered.

My blood was boiling but it was Thumper who spoke up.

"Let me tell you something, Buck. God doesn't make mistakes."

Buck stared at him. It looked as if he was really listening.

"I've got one," he said. "What do you call a gay drive-by shooting?"

Lewis stood up. "If you don't shut your mouth, Buck, I'm going to shut it for you."

Buck looked around. "Anyone?"

He grinned. "A fruit rollup. Get it?"

Lewis lunged toward him.

"Lewis," said Thumper. "Stop."

Buck rolled his eyes. "What are you going to do, mate? Karate chop me to death?"

Lewis grabbed him by the collar and shoved him to the ground. Miracle burrowed into me, her thumb in her mouth and her eyes closed.

Thumper pulled himself shakily to standing. He stood between them.

"Buck, it's time you moved on. I wish you peace."

I could see them, the tears that filled Buck's eyes.

But he wouldn't let up.

"A piece of what?" he said.

When no one reacted he packed up and left. I stared at a loose thread on Lewis's sleeping bag. I wanted to pull it until I unraveled.

"Sorry, Poppy," said Thumper. "It was the right thing to do."

"I know," I said.

Lewis whispered in Miracle's ear. "I think Thumper needs a cuddle."

Then he took my hand. "Let's walk."

We made our way alongside the river.

"The answer," he said, "is to get to the other side."

"The answer to what?"

"Why the chicken crossed the road."

"Yeah, well, my road is full of car crashes. And Buck is the biggest one of all."

He nodded to a clearing near the water. "Let's sit."

I sat on a boulder. Lewis sat on one a couple of feet away.

It was dark but I could see stones embedded in the mud at my feet. I loosened them with my heel. We sat in silence. The river trickled and the bushes rustled in the breeze. Lewis cleared his throat. I could see, out of the corner of my eye, his hand stretched toward mine. I reached out and held it. We sat there, linked, like a pair of figures in a paper-doll chain.

"I can use my money," he said. "To buy you a big

bulldozer. You could scrape up all of the crashes and throw them in the dump."

I smiled. "That would be nice. But I still wouldn't know how."

"How to what?" he asked.

I turned to look at him. "How to get to the other side."

"Rule number one," he said. "Always cross with a buddy."

I moved to his boulder. He put his arm around me. I thought about Cam, about what his road was like. I wondered if I was the wreck in the middle of it.

After a while Lewis stood up. "Let's head back."

I led the way.

～～

Mom was dozing on the couch. She was curled up on her side and there was this gap between her elbows and her knees that I was desperate to fill.

She opened her eyes. "You okay?"

"No."

She patted the spot. I sat in it.

"Lie down if you want."

"Okay."

I faced away from her. I hated how stiff I was.

She stroked my hair.

"You'll be back to school in a couple of weeks."

I closed my eyes. "Yeah."

"Are you ready?"

I laughed. "No."

She put her arm around my waist.

"Cam will be okay, you know. Promise."

I let myself settle against the warmth of her body.

I didn't wake until morning.

I went to the pharmacy and bought a hot-water bottle. I filled it at the drop-in center. I watched him sleep for a few minutes before placing the bottle next to his hip.

He opened his eyes. "What's this?"

"It's for your arthritis."

His eyes went watery.

"Thank you, Poppy."

I helped him sit up.

"How's your brother?" he asked.

"It's like half of me is missing."

"Don't worry," he said. "You'll be whole again."

"Maybe," I said. "But it won't be the same. It's like when your ice cream falls off the cone and lands on the ground. You can pick it up and put it back on, but it'll be messy and covered in shit."

He laughed. "Interesting analogy. But here's a better

one. Think of a broken vase that's been fixed. Sure, there's a huge crack running down the center of it, but there's a thick layer of superglue too—and that makes the vase stronger than ever."

I didn't want a big, ugly crack between me and Cam.

"I want to show you something," he said.

He pulled up the sleeve of his T-shirt. "This is the glue the holds me together."

I ran my fingers across the tattoo. *R.I.P. Rodrigo.*

For a second I wondered if Thumper was coming out to me.

"Who's Rodrigo?"

"My cellmate." He let his sleeve drop. "He saved my life."

He moved the hot-water bottle to his knee. "I used to be half a person too, Poppy. Less than half. A quarter. An eighth. A sixteenth. Hell, I was barely human."

He opened his mouth to say more, then shut it again.

"You don't have to talk about it," I said. "If you don't want to."

"I hated him," he said. "Because he was Latino. I gave him a hard time, cornering him, threatening him. His response was always the same. *I don't want to fight you, brother.*"

I pictured a bony old hand on a tiny, sweet shoulder. I inched in closer until we were touching. Then I rested my head on his shoulder.

"The other Latinos, they got tired of my bullshit. They beat me to a pulp in the courtyard one day. They'd have killed me if it wasn't for Rodrigo. He was my human shield."

I placed my hand on his arm, my fingertips just under his shirt.

"Afterwards, in our cell, he became my healer. He cleaned my wounds and dressed them with strips of cloth he tore from his bedsheet."

Watering eyes, it seemed, were contagious.

"I'd been stuck in a hole, Poppy. A pit of hate. Rodrigo pulled me out."

I wondered if I'd been in a pit too.

"It was his stories," he said. "About his *abuela* and the country he came from. Seeing him as human made me more human."

He put his hand over mine, squeezed it as tight as an arthritic hand could. "That's when I wrote my bible. I preached to anyone who would listen. They called me Bible Thumper."

I felt proud. It was amazing how much one man could change.

I linked my arm around his. "I'd put my hand in fire for you, Thumper."

His voice was a whisper. "Thank you, Poppy."

We sat quietly and when Thumper's eyes began to close

I eased him back down onto his blankets. I kissed his cheek goodbye.

Before I left I looked in the snub tub.

And immediately wished that I hadn't.

⟡

Miracle and her mom were reading on the couch. They waved me in.

"Is Lewis here?"

"Upstairs," said her mom. "First door on the right."

He looked startled to see me.

I passed him the note. "It's from Buck."

He read it aloud. "'This is who I am. Sorry.'"

He looked up. "What the hell?"

We sat side by side at his desk. Lewis typed in the website address Buck had included in the note.

www.buckleytwhittingham.co.uk

A photo appeared on the screen. The caption underneath read *Buckley at home.* He was sitting on a chrome barstool in front of a floor-to-ceiling painting of a naked woman.

Our eyes scanned the page.

Buckley immigrated to Canada when his mother, Dr. Flora Whittingham, received a top research position at one of Canada's most prestigious universities. Buckley's interest in photography started at an early age. His work has shown in galleries throughout the U.K. Click here to see Buckley's most recent collection: Life in the Concrete Jungle.

I was stunned.

We both were.

Another photo—Buck in the doorway of an abandoned building, his arm around a dog's neck. Underneath, a quote: *To really capture life on the streets I lived for several months as a homeless youth. It has all at once been exciting, wonderful, and heartbreaking. Enjoy!*

Lewis looked at me. I nodded. He hit the "next" button.

The first photo was of Thumper, reading his bible under the bridge. It was called "Criminal Contemplation."

The "add to cart" button made me sick.

"He said *enjoy*," I said. "As if he was selling cotton candy. Or movie tickets."

We clicked through the gallery. Many of the photos I'd already seen—the old lady smoking a cigarette, the girl kicking the beer can down the alley. They all had heartbreaking captions.

I pushed my chair away from the computer and moved to the bed.

I leaned against the headboard and stared at the ceiling.

"You okay?" said Lewis.

"No."

I glanced back at the computer screen. Thumper was brushing his teeth near the river. A private moment, exploited.

I knew there'd be more. I'd be there. And Miracle. I wondered how much he charged for us.

Lewis sat beside me and put an arm around me.

"It's okay," he said. "You can cry."

I turned into him, put my arms around his waist and my head on his shoulder. But I couldn't cry. I was numb.

"Lewis?"

"Yeah?"

"Have you ever asked yourself, *What's the point?*"

He shook his head. "I don't ask myself stupid questions."

"How is that a stupid question?" I asked.

"Everyone says '*the* point.' As if there's just one thing that makes life worth living. But the point is lots of things."

"Like what?" I asked.

"For me it's who I was and who I am and who I'll be. It's everything I know and everything I don't know. It's this, right here, right now."

I laid my hand on his chest. "You're amazing."

I thought about his surgeries, the one he'd had and the one he needed.

"I'm going to talk to Buck," I said. "Demand that he give us whatever money he earns from our photos. We can put it toward your surgery."

He smiled. "Thanks. But I have money from my dad, remember?"

"No you don't," I said. "You spent it on a bulldozer."

He laughed. "I did?"

"Yep. I used it to scoop Buck up. He's in the dump now, where he belongs."

"Good," he said. "I'm glad."

"Yeah," I said. "Me too."

CHAPTER NINE

Miracle was eating chicken wings at the counter. Her cheeks were stained with tears.

"Where's Mr. Chen?" I asked.

She nodded to the back.

He was sitting in a chair in the corner.

I'd never seen him sitting before. Poor man was overworked. And having Miracle around all the time probably didn't help.

Before I had a chance to ask him why she'd been crying he said, "Do you like this job, Poppy Flower?"

"Of course," I said. "Otherwise I wouldn't do it."

"What do you like about it?" he said. "Besides the hiding?"

"Hiding?" I said, through the mesh screen in my neck. "I don't know what you are talking about."

"You wear your costume to and from work," he said. "I've never had a mascot do that before."

"It gets me in character," I said.

Mr. Chen rolled his eyes. "Oh, please."

"If you don't think this job is suitable for me," I said, grooming my chest feathers, "you can always fire me."

"That's not what I'm saying," he said. "I just think you might want to reflect on why you chose this job and whether or not you're happy."

"I'm happy," I said. "Deliriously happy."

He rolled his eyes. "Excuse me while I get my mop. There's a puddle forming from your dripping sarcasm."

"None of this really matters anyway," I said. "Summer's coming to an end and this mascot gig will be a thing of the past."

He looked to the sky. "Hallelujah."

For some reason, I didn't feel as jubilant as he did.

"Anyway," I said, "I just came back here to ask about Miracle. She looks upset."

"The social worker's car was outside her house," he said. "She's afraid they've come to take her away."

"Do you think they will?" I asked.

He shook his head. "I don't know."

We headed back to the front counter. Miracle was gone.

"I wish her mother would do a better job of keeping an eye on her," I said.

"It takes a village, Poppy Flower."

"Where's the village when she's down on James Street with the drug addicts and the crazy people?"

"James Street *is* the village," he said. "Part of it anyway."

"James Street? A village?" I said. "Pfssh. More like a slum. If you ask me, that place needs cleaning up."

"It's not cleaning it needs," said Mr. Chen. "It's fixing. I've been fighting for a long time for more services down there, to get the police focused on harm reduction, not law enforcement, to open more health clinics."

Tears pricked my eyes. "It's just as well I spend my time hiding," I said. "I don't think I'm a very nice person."

"Don't worry, Poppy Flower," he said. "You might be completely useless as a chicken, but as humans go I think you're pretty fine."

He wasn't so bad himself.

I looked at the till. "Remember that night I worked on cash?"

He picked up a cloth and started wiping the counter. "Yes. I remember."

I reached for the cloth and took over his cleaning. "Remember how I answered the phone?"

He put on a feminine voice. "*Chen Chicken. Poppy speaking. How may I be of service?*"

I laughed. "That was very professional of me, wasn't it?"

He shrugged. "I suppose."

I kept my head down and scrubbed a particularly stubborn coffee stain. "Mr. Chen, I was wondering if, in the fall—"

He reached over, put his hand gently on mine. "Yes."

I looked up. "Really?"

He slid the cloth from under my hand. "As long as you keep up with your studies."

He looked at the stain with disgust.

"Try whiskey," I said. "I heard it really does the trick."

He pointed to the door. "Out."

I smiled. "I won't let you down, Mr. Chen."

Outside, I marched with my sign up and down the street. A car pulled up. An old man inside it said, "You selling sex?"

"No," I said. "Chicken wings."

He looked me up and down. "How much?"

I pointed to the sign. "$8.99 a dozen."

He parked the car and went into the shop.

Guess I wasn't so useless after all.

Things were quiet at the bridge that night. It was just the two of us, Thumper and me. There was a hole in my life but he filled it a bit. But then Lewis rounded the corner and the hole got a little bit bigger.

"Miracle's gone."

Butterflies filled my stomach.

"Her mom thought she was in her room but she wasn't. We've looked everywhere."

"She left Chen Chicken at four," I said.

I counted on my fingers. "That was four hours ago."

"Have the police been called?" said Thumper.

He nodded. "They're on the way."

Images flashed in my mind. Nasty, horrible, vile images.

I ran to the river and threw up. "She's dead," I said. "Someone kidnapped her. They did terrible things, then they killed her."

Lewis grabbed me by the arms. "Get a grip, Poppy."

"I can't," I said.

"You can," he said. "And you will."

⟿

We went to Miracle's house. Prints of her latest school photo covered the kitchen table. The cops wanted to speak with me. They wanted to know what Miracle was last seen wearing, but all I could picture was Miracle dead in a ditch—a beautiful mix of pattern and color dumped in a pile of dirt.

My voice shook.

"Her baby-blue shirt was covered in hearts and her backpack was dotted *and* striped. She wore her hair in two braided buns, high on her head like mouse ears. Her skirt was green with three tiers of frills and there was a Band-Aid on her right knee. Her Mary Jane shoes had lights in the soles and her socks had polka dots."

I felt an officer's hand on my shoulder. "'Don't worry, about a thing.'"

He said *thing* without the *h*.

꯬

Cam was staring at the ceiling with headphones on. I took them off with shaking hands.

"The little girl with the polka-dot socks, she's gone missing."

"Go away, Poppy."

"This is serious," I said.

"You know what else is serious?" he said. "A little thing called a sexual assault evidence kit. You'll be happy to know that my genital bruising has been thoroughly documented."

My head was spinning. I leaned against his wall.

"Sorry," he said. "Am I boring you?"

"No. I—"

"I know this isn't as exciting as a missing kid," he said, "but it's kind of a big deal to me."

My voice came out strangled. "She's all on her own."

"Don't be so dramatic, Poppy. Little kids are always

getting up to no good. She'll be home in a few hours, when her little adventure gets old."

I grabbed hold of his words, clung to them for dear life. "Oh, Cam. Do you really think so?"

He put his headphones back on. "I dunno. Maybe. What the hell do I know?"

Miracle was dead and Cam hated me. What was the point if my points were all gone?

~~~

I cried in my mom's arms. My dad put me to bed like I was a child. I wanted to search all night, but he said no, he wanted me home safe and sound. So I stayed in bed, but when he was gone I jumped into a portal of darkness.

I watched kidnappings caught on tape.

What if she was gone? What if I never saw her again?

I went to Buck's website, scoured for photos of Miracle. There were many.

Miracle, in her sleeping bag under the bridge.

Miracle, throwing stones into the river.

Miracle, mid-pirouette.

The images were beautiful. The captions were not.

No fixed address.

Passing time at the homeless camp.

Street girl dancing.

Buck was selling a lie.

I scrolled through hundreds of photos.

One took my breath away. It was Lewis, his head in Thumper's lap, his tearstained face looking into mine. Devastated, yet hopeful.

I put my head on my pillow. I pictured Miracle in all her clatching glory.

I couldn't wait to see her again.

A breeze flowed in through my window. I hoped it would carry my sadness to Cam so he would come back to me.

I woke up at six. I went under the bridge to see if Miracle was there. Thumper was reading his bible. He said there'd been some news.

I ran home, pressed my face to Cam's door. It was cold against my cheek.

"They found a shoe."

He didn't answer.

My voice was broken. "It had lights in the sole."

I went to see Lewis. His hopeful face looked into mine. "We'll find her."

We searched the part of the river where the shoe was found. We looked through the overgrown weeds and fallen trees. We were startled by a rustling beside us. I grabbed Lewis's hand. Maybe it was her. Maybe she'd been lost in the woods. The tall grass parted. It was Cam. He ran to me. We touched foreheads. We wiped each other's tears with our thumbs.

Then we continued the search.

The three of us went back to Miracle's. The house was full of people—neighbors, Mr. Chen, business owners from Elgin and James. Thumper was sitting on the couch. He had his bible in his lap. I touched it, hoping something profound would seep from the pages into my soul.

She hadn't been seen in nineteen hours. My stomach was churning. The butterflies were gone and in their place were miniature dragons, breathing fire and jabbing my insides.

Miracle's mom was standing in the kitchen. Someone was holding her hand while a police officer asked questions. She said, "I don't know. I'm sorry. I can't think straight."

I knew the problem. She was frozen inside a big block of ice.

Mr. Chen dinged a teacup to get everyone's attention. He didn't look worried anymore—he looked determined. He said the police were doing their best but we had the manpower of a small army. He spread out a map on the kitchen table and divided the downtown core into sections. Lewis, Cam, and I said we'd take James, because Lewis knew it well.

Just as we were getting ready to leave, Buck showed up.

"Get lost, Buck," said Lewis. "We don't need your help."

Cam got in his face. "Anyone who calls my sister the Pillsbury Doughboy is asking for a knuckle sandwich."

Buck brushed past us. "You can give it to me later, mate. After we've found Miracle."

Miracle's mom fell into his arms when she saw him. "She's been gone so long."

A house full of people and it was Buck who melted the ice.

"I told her that you were helping with the rent," she said, "that I didn't need to work anymore. But she was still scared that she'd be taken away."

Buck rubbed her shoulders. "Look at all these people. They're going to find her."

The search parties began heading out.

We were just getting ready when I saw Buck looking at Mr. Chen's map. He was all alone.

I caught his eye. "Well, come on if you're coming."

We walked, all four of us, down the tracks toward James Street.

"What if she was hit by a train?" I said.

"She wasn't hit by a train," said Buck.

I saw a photo once. Of a dismembered body.

"What if we only find part of her?"

"Pops," said Cam. "Stop."

Lewis took my hand. "Don't worry," he said. "She'll be back before you know it, twerking inappropriately and driving you nuts."

That's when it hit me.

"Oh my God."

I took off like a bat out of hell.

"What the hell, Pops?"

"Slow down, Pidge."

I ran down Elgin with the others on my heels. When I got to James, I caught my breath with my hands on my knees.

I looked between two second-story windows. Was it the room above the tattoo parlor? Or the room above Massage and More?

"Pops," said Cam. "What's going on?"

"MaJonna," I said. "She's with MaJonna."

He frowned. "Who the hell is MaJonna?"

"MaJonna?" said Lewis. "Why didn't you say?"

He ran to the door next to Massage and More and tried the handle.

I looked at him, surprised. "You know MaJonna?"

He thumped the door open with his shoulder. "Everyone knows MaJonna."

We scrambled up the stairs to Madonna's "Vogue." The first thing I saw when we stepped into the apartment was a six-foot-tall man in a blond wig and a cone bra. Next to him, with two waffle cones taped to her T-shirt, was Miracle. They were in the middle of a choreographed routine. She smiled when she saw us, like a child in a school play who'd just spotted her parents. I made a move for her but Lewis held me back. "Let them finish," he whispered. "She's safe. He's harmless."

While they performed, Buck called Miracle's mother. When the song was over we clapped, some of us more enthusiastically than others.

"Bravo, bravo," shouted Cam.

I rushed to Miracle and hugged her, squashing her cone bra to bits. "You've had us all worried sick!"

I was shaking, with anger, relief, and confusion. Miracle, on the other hand, was pretty relaxed.

"I came for a sleepover," she said, "so I could learn to dance like a pro. If I get famous I can take care of Mama."

MaJonna hugged Lewis hard. "Lewis the lunch man!"

Lewis smiled. "Okay, Jon. Not so tight."

I looked at Lewis. "Lunch man?"

"I volunteer with a lunch program on Saturdays," he said.

I needed to brush up on my connecting skills. "You do?"

MaJonna moved on to Buck. "Camera man!"

"Hey, mate," said Buck. "How's that new CD player working out?"

He was an asshole, but a generous one.

We heard sirens in the distance.

MaJonna looked frightened. "Am I in trouble?"

Cam stepped in. "Hey, MaJonna. What's your favorite Madonna song? Mine's 'Like a Prayer.'"

MaJonna riddled off his top twenty, from best to worst.

Lewis looked to Buck. "They won't arrest him, will they?"

Buck shook his head. "I hope not."

Miracle's mom burst through the door. She fell to her knees, grabbed her daughter, and held her tight. She cried like I'd never heard anyone cry before. It was a wailing, from somewhere down deep. It made Miracle cry too. "I'm sorry, Mama. I'm sorry."

MaJonna hugged the officers. He knew them all by name. My officer was Ben.

Miracle seemed confused by the officer's questions. "Why would he hurt me? I slept on his couch. He only got mad once, when he forgot the words to 'Express Yourself.'"

A caseworker showed up. She reminded MaJonna about responsibility. She said if he couldn't make good choices, he'd be moved to a group home. He slammed his fist on the table. Then he sobbed. "I'm sorry. I didn't mean it. I won't do it again." Officer Ben got him a glass of water. "Come on, Jon. Calm down, you're alright."

Lewis squeezed MaJonna's shoulder. "Don't cry, buddy."

Buck held Miracle so her mom could hold MaJonna's hand.

Cam and I stood back. The whole scene was beautifully sad.

⟶

Miracle's house was full of people. Search parties returned to food and drink, put together by the shopkeepers of Elgin and James.

Mr. Chen bawled when he saw his Merry-girl. I had to go to the bathroom to pull myself together. When I left the bathroom Buck was waiting outside.

"Can we talk?"

"You stole our stories."

"Those photos are art."

"I agree," I said. "But did you have to lie? Pretend to be homeless? Why couldn't you just come down to the bridge, say, *Hi, I'm a photographer, may I take your picture?*"

He didn't speak. Not because he was at a loss for words

but because he was full of them and didn't know where to begin.

I nodded to the back door. We went outside and sat on the steps.

"The thing is, Pidge, I've been alone my whole life. My parents divorced when I was five, my mom had her career. I had photography but it wasn't enough. I wanted to be someone different."

"So you slummed it under the bridge?"

"I wanted something more. I wanted to feel . . . I don't know . . . fulfilled."

"You think homelessness is fulfilling?"

He shrugged. "More fulfilling than that sterile, empty apartment my mother set me up in."

I snorted. "It didn't look empty to me," I said. "*Isaac* had shitloads of stuff."

His face turned pink. "They're just things, Pidge. Thumper has more than I do. And he has nothing."

I stole a sideways glance at him. He looked empty, like a bag of skin filled with organs and bones.

"I was jealous," he said. "You, Thumper, Lewis, and Miracle—you're all good. And I'm not. It's not that I'm bad, it's that I'm weak. I wish that wasn't the case, but it is."

I felt bad for him because I knew how he felt. I wasn't that good either—but I was getting better. I wished I knew how to help him, to make him stronger. But that was a road he'd have to cross himself. Too bad he had to go it alone. After all, rule number one is, always cross with a buddy.

He ran his fingers through his hair. It went all swoopy on the top. "You can go get that brother of yours to give me a knuckle sandwich if you want."

I laughed. "There'll be no need for that."

He smiled. "I really did fancy you."

He had charm, oodles of it.

I smiled. "I know."

He moved to the backyard gate.

"Buck?"

"Yeah."

"You put that hundred-dollar bill in the tin for Lewis's surgery, didn't you?"

He smiled. "He's a great guy."

"Yeah," I said, "he is."

He was almost out of the yard when I said, "Did the money mean anything to you? I'm just wondering because, well . . . the rent, the money for Lewis . . . they're big gestures . . . but are they a sacrifice?"

He looked hurt by the question. "They made a difference to the people who received them," he said. "Isn't that enough?"

I thought of Miracle's three dollars and forty-five cents.

"I don't know," I said. "Is it?"

He stared off into the distance, then closed the gate between us.

"Take care, Pidge."

Then he was gone.

I looked at the wooden fence around the perimeter.

I remembered back to the beginning, when Buck had recited Tramp's speech about life off the leash, about the world being a place of fun and adventure. *Don't fence yourself in, Pidge.*

I stood up and brushed myself off. I liked Miracle's yard. Maybe we could all pitch in and get her a swing set or a sandbox or a slide. Living life off the leash may have its benefits, but I figured a six-year-old could do with a little fencing in.

⟿

Cam and Lewis were hitting it off over a sandwich platter. Cam raised his eyebrows at me. I'd tell him to keep his hands off later.

I went to the living room. Miracle was sitting cross-legged in Thumper's lap. Thumper held one of her little feet in his hand.

I sat beside them, tweaked one of her toes. "How did you lose your shoes?"

"I took them off during my dance lesson."

"What dance lesson?"

"The one in the river."

Thumper and I exchanged a glance. "You had a dance lesson in the river?"

"Just up to our ankles. MaJonna said it was good for balance. He said it was good to feel mud between your toes."

"That's cool," I said. "But why didn't you put your shoes back on afterwards?"

"MaJonna wasn't wearing any and I want to be just like him."

I smiled. "You do?"

"He's going to build me a ladder so I can reach for the stars."

Thumper chuckled. "And I'll bet you'll climb it too," he said. "Two rungs at a time."

His old, wrinkled hand, her baby-smooth foot. It made my heart swell.

I leaned over, kissed Miracle on the forehead. "I'm glad you're home, Miracle."

Cam and I headed home. He told me he liked my friends. I said they could be his friends too. Cam and me, we shared everything.

Frank was in front of his house, painting his picket fence. "Where's Ralph?" I asked.

He looked surprised. "What do you think," he said, "we just sit here all day talking about the price of gas?"

My face reddened with shame. "No," I said. "Of course not."

He nodded back to Ralph's house. "He's putting his wife to bed. She needs lots of help, you know, with the dementia."

I had been so obsessed with the bad side of people, I'd been imagining it in people who were good.

I wasn't sure what to say so Cam spoke for me. He always had my back. "Let Ralph know we're thinking of him. Okay?"

Mom and Dad said they'd heard the news. They wanted to take us out to celebrate but we just wanted our beds.

"Tomorrow?" they said.

Cam and I smiled. "Tomorrow."

We parted on the landing.

"That Lewis," he said, swooning. "Man."

"Yeah," I said. "And he's all mine."

The next day, Mom and Dad went out so we could have the house to ourselves. We spent hours in our little living room, setting up a backdrop with the bright-yellow bed-sheet from the Salvation Army store and using various lamps to get the lighting just right.

Cam and Lewis took turns with the camera.

I re-created the pose, my modernized version with the skinny jeans and red Converse boots as well as the 1942 original with the denim workshirt.

I wanted some pinup shots too, which Lewis was more than happy to take. I wore a vintage striped bikini and played around with a variety of poses. I lay on my stomach with my legs crossed in the air behind me, my chin on my hands. In another I bent slightly forward, one hand on my waist, the other holding a tube of lipstick to my mouth.

Lewis started sounding like a professional photographer. "Beautiful, Poppy. Gorgeous. Hot."

Cam told us to get a room.

I changed into a vintage dress. I posed in a chair, legs crossed and back arched, the skirt of my dress raised just above my garter belt and thigh-high stockings. Lewis almost lost his mind.

"One more outfit," I said.

I went upstairs.

When I came back down Cam tweaked my beak. "This getup never gets old."

Lewis took the photo. I wondered if Mr. Chen would

hang it in his shop. Me in my chicken suit, wing flexed, a red bandana on my feathery head.

Cam said I was amazing. He left the room and when he came back I was blown away. His chest was beautifully bronzed and his shorts matched the blue of his perfectly lined eyes. His head protection obscured much of his face but his red-painted lips popped.

The best part of all was his craptacular heels.

My sweet Cam.

He was the eyeliner queen and the boxing king all at once.

꙾

After the photo shoot, Lewis and I went to my room. He asked to see my entire vintage clothes collection so I tried them on, every last piece. Lewis zipped the zips and buttoned the buttons. He did everything slowly and I was glad. I liked his touch and I wanted it to last. We could have gone farther, as far as I liked, but I knew our time would come. And when it did he wouldn't need to ask if it was tender enough. It just would be.

My final outfit was a deliberate choice. A denim button-down shirt paired with high-waisted shorts. Lewis tied my shirttails into a knot at my ribcage. I breathed in deeply and exhaled fully. My internal organs were safe and sound. Cam would be glad.

I patted my bed. Connections were all well and good but they had to be tight. Loose connections were garbled and fuzzy.

Lewis sat beside me.

I said, "Cam says people lose their shit about where transgender people pee."

He leaned back against the headboard. "I had to use the staff bathroom in high school because a bunch of parents complained."

"Complained about what?" I asked.

"What was in my pants," he said.

I frowned. "How did they know what was in your pants?"

"My dad told the principal. It was an innocent mistake. He should have just told them I was having my tonsils out."

Poor Lewis. The thoughts in his brain were a tangle of wires.

He smiled. "Sorry. I'm not explaining this very well."

I nestled into him. I hoped my head on his shoulder and my arm around his waist would help the wires unravel.

"I lied to you," he said.

My heart skipped a beat. "You did?"

"I went to your school," he said. "Before my transition."

I immediately tried to imagine him as he was then, to feminize his strong and angular face so that I might recall a time when our paths had crossed. Then I stopped myself. He was Lewis now. That was what mattered.

"I'm sorry," he said. "I should have mentioned it. It's just—ninth grade was a crazy-ass year. I wasn't who I am now and—"

I squeezed his arm. "You don't need to explain."

He went quiet for a bit, his eyes fixed thoughtfully on my Rosie poster.

"There's this photo of me in a dress," he said. "I look like a hostage. It's as if, just out of the shot, there's a kidnapper holding a gun to my head. My eyes are pleading to the camera—*Get me out of this getup, please. Pay the ransom, no matter how much it is.* I was four."

He laughed to himself. "It's pretty funny, actually, how uncomfortable I looked. My grandmother had insisted on the photo. The next day my mother took me shopping. She brought me to the boys' department, asked if there was anything I liked. She was cool like that. A year later, she was hit by a car because sometimes life is cruel. My father bought me a waistcoat and tie for her funeral. He was cool like that too."

"So they knew?" I said. "Way back then?"

"Kind of," he said. "But not really."

I glanced up at him. I could almost see the wires untangling in his brain.

"You know how some parents expect their daughters to be girlie girls?" he said. "Well, my parents weren't like that. They saw me as a tomboy so I saw myself that way too. I liked who I was. Until I started developing. Then I hated myself. With every physical change I lost a bit of who I was. I felt robbed somehow. Of who I was supposed to be. The girls in my class, they celebrated their changes— their first bras, their first periods. I felt guilty, because I wasn't celebrating. I was mourning—which was weird, because how can you mourn something you never had?"

I reached for his hand, gave it a squeeze.

"The worst part was getting my period," he said. "When my dad gave the cashier $4.99 for my first box of Kotex I burst out crying—like that one transaction was sealing my fate or something. Poor Dad, he was so confused. He took me out for ice cream after, rambled on about the wonders of puberty. He said that each period was something to be thankful for, that each one was a symbol of my womanhood. That's when I told him that I was never, ever, going to be a woman, no matter how many glorious periods I had. He went quiet, for a real long time. Then he took a piece of paper out of his pocket and said, 'Well, I guess I won't be needing this.' He ripped it up into a million pieces."

"What was it?" I asked.

Lewis grinned. "Cheat notes on how to talk to girls about their periods. My aunt had written it for him."

I laughed. "Your dad was the best."

Lewis nodded in agreement. "He took me to the family doctor after that and got me a referral to a gender dysphoria specialist. I had counseling all through eighth grade and into ninth grade. I learned that everyone transitions in different ways, but for me, I knew it had to be medically. Dad supported me one hundred percent. When I said I wanted to go on testosterone he scrimped and saved to pay for my treatments. When I said I wanted top surgery he got me on a waiting list. All of these things he did because he didn't want me to be a hostage again. He wanted me to be free."

From the corner of my eye I could see the tears welling in his eyes.

"Soon I had things to celebrate too," he said. "A deeper voice, facial hair, a squarer jaw."

I reached up, traced the outline of his face with my fingers.

"I was changing," he said. "But what I didn't know was that my dad was changing too. When he told me about the cancer I changed my name to Lewis. I thought that by choosing his name he'd live longer. Stupid, huh?"

I moved my hand from his face to his chest. I could feel the *thump-thump-thump* of his heart.

"It's not stupid," I said. "It's beautiful."

Lewis laid his hand gently on mine. "Shortly after his diagnosis I started tenth grade at Westvale. It started off really well—I was living my life as it was meant to be lived and Dad was responding well to treatment. But that spring, things went downhill. Dad didn't think twice about telling the principal why I would be off for two weeks. He thought surely she'd keep my surgery confidential."

I looked up. "She didn't?"

Lewis shook his head. "She said she told the staff for my own protection—whatever that meant. It wasn't long before everyone knew I was transgender and the bathroom thing became a huge deal. There was even a petition to keep me out of the boys' room. When I complained to the principal about how unfair it all was she said, 'All this fuss. Wouldn't it be easier if you just became a lesbian?'"

I cringed. "That's horrible."

"Yes," he said. "It was. But it's over now. And I'm stronger for it."

I lay quietly, thinking about all he'd just said.

"Lewis?"

"Yeah?"

"I understand why you changed schools," I said. "But I wish you'd stayed at Pearson High. If anyone started a petition I'd have started a counter one—I'd have fought for your rights. I'd have been your number one supporter."

I'd have probably blundered my way through it but at least I'd have stepped up.

At least I hoped I would have.

Lewis laughed. "Yeah. You'd have brought it to the attention of the whole student body during one of the assemblies."

I eyed him suspiciously. "You remember me?"

"Of course," he said. "You and your brother emceed all the events."

It was my turn to go quiet.

"What's wrong?" he asked.

I propped myself up on my elbow and looked down at him. "I feel . . . I dunno . . . jealous. You got to know me before I got to know you."

"I didn't *know* you," he said. "We never said two words to each other. I just saw you onstage a few times. It's no big deal."

He was right but I couldn't help but feel put out.

He reached up and touched my cheek. "I wish I never mentioned it now," he said. "I didn't mean to make you sad."

"I'm not sad," I said. "It's just—if I had met you back then maybe you would have told me about yourself and maybe I would have been there for you every step of the way and maybe what we have now, we could have had this whole time."

He laughed. "There you go, overthinking things again."

"Seriously though," I said. "Just think about it. Maybe one day I dropped something in the hallway and you picked it up and maybe we actually touched."

He moved his hand to the small of my back, the tips of his fingers inside the waistband of my jeans. "We're actually touching now."

I bent down, put my face close to his. "Yes. We are."

I kissed his lips, then settled back into his arms.

He pulled me close and looked back at Rosie.

"I can see why you like her," he said. "She kind of bridges the gap between masculine and feminine."

I slipped my hand inside his shirt and kissed him, from the base of his neck to his ear. "Yes," I said. "She's pretty cool."

Early the next morning I stood at my window breathing in the late summer air. I could see Ralph sitting in his garden drinking what I imagined to be instant coffee, the just-add-hot-water kind that came in a jar.

I leaned on the windowsill and had a good hard look at him. He ran his hand over his face like he'd just walked through a cobweb and was wiping it off.

I watched him bring his mug to his lips. For all I knew he went to the trendiest coffee shop in town and bought fresh beans that he ground at home with a fancy grinder.

When Ralph finished his drink, he cradled the empty mug in his hands and gazed into it as if he wished it would magically refill itself.

I wondered what it would be like to have so much weighing heavily on your mind.

I closed the window and went to my closet. I changed from my pajamas to a pair of short denim overalls with a white cotton crop top underneath. I looked in the mirror and applied my makeup in my usual forties style. I penciled in my naturally arched brows, plumped up my lashes with dark mascara, and liberally applied rouge to my cheeks. I reached for my bandana. Once it was tied around my head I painted my lips with Cam's Chanel Rouge Allure.

Twenty minutes later I was at the arena. The doors were locked but I'd known they would be. I knocked until Eddie answered. He took one look at the skates slung over my shoulder and said, "You've got a half hour before the public skate starts."

I sat at the edge of the rink and laced up. I stared at my feet for two whole minutes before I stood up.

I started to skate. Slowly at first, but then I picked up speed until the space around me blurred, but in a good way. It felt good. I was tired of sharpening the focus, zooming in, making things bigger than they were.

Life whirled around me. The good and the bad spun through the air, twisting and tumbling like debris in a tornado. I knew that when I slowed the dust would settle and something bad might land right in my face, but that was okay—all I'd have to do was start skating again, and the debris would lift off and life would whirl once again.

A sweat broke out in the small of my back. If I was in my chicken suit I'd be cursing but this was different. The sweat rolling down my butt wasn't a consequence of poor working conditions—it was a reward for hard work. I'd earned that sweat and I wanted more.

A flash of green popped from the blur, again and again and again. Then, a voice.

"You want some music?"

I slowed to a reluctant glide. It was Eve, cross-legged on top of the concessions counter.

I smiled. "You choose."

She reached behind the counter. A moment later, Queen filled the arena.

I burst out laughing.

"Go on," she said. "Skate."

I was Mrs. Fahrenheit alright. I was two hundred degrees of hot shit. Was I turning the world inside out? Probably not. The world was the world.

I looked over at Eve. She was eating popcorn and watching my every move. Next to her were two slushies. One had my name written all over it. Literally. In lime-green Sharpie.

I had only come for a casual skate, to get back into the groove, but with the music pumping and Eve watching I decided to give it my all. I combined my chicken moves with my skating skills. I hopped and I skipped and

I jumped. I shimmy-shimmy-kicked and I wiggled my butt. I grapevined and did a kick-ass pirouette. As the song approached its end I knew what I had to do—I slid across the rink on my knees and collapsed in a dramatic heap. I stayed there for a good thirty seconds after the song ended. The effect was staggering. Moments later so was I. Eve helped me hobble off the rink.

"And this," she said, "is why we wear kneepads when we skate."

"It was supposed to be a casual practice," I said. "Just to get back into the groove."

She sat me down at the snack bar and gave me ice for my right knee, which was already beginning to bruise.

"And here's a slushie," she said. "It has your name on it. Literally."

It was like we were psychic or something.

I raised my cup in the air. "To good friends."

She squinted at my eyes. "You know, this classic forties aesthetic you've got going on is verging on boring. Maybe try some colored liner. Or some darker shadow."

I raised my slushie up higher. "*Eve.*"

She smiled, picked up her cup, and tapped it against mine. "To good friends."

While I took a long drink, she pulled the lime-green Sharpie out of her pocket and popped the lid off.

"What are you doing with that?" I asked.

She leaned forward. "Lining your eyes in a more dramatic fashion."

I pulled back. "Not with indelible ink you're not."

"Taylor Swift did it once," she said. "During a makeup emergency on a plane."

I grabbed the marker and put the lid back on it. "Well then, Taylor Swift is a friggin' nutbar."

She slipped the Sharpie back into her pocket. "Maybe I could bring my makeup kit over sometime," she said. "I'd be happy to try to make you look less boring."

I leaned forward, took a good long hard look at her. It was as if someone had dipped a paintbrush into rust-colored paint and, with a gentle flick of the wrist, added a sprinkling of character across her face.

I smiled. "I'd like that."

I settled on my bed with my leg rested on a pillow. Cam came in with an icepack.

"I called Mr. Chen. He said you always did strike him as a skiver."

I laughed. "What's a skiver?"

Cam put the icepack gently on my knee. "Someone who skips work, I think."

I patted the bed. "Stay awhile?"

He got comfy beside me.

"Thanks for helping with the photo shoot," I said.

"You're welcome, Pops."

I pictured him in his headgear and heels.

"Go on," he said. "Ask. I know you want to."

He could read me like a book. "Do you think you'll go back to boxing?"

He smiled. "Promise you won't be mad?"

"Mad about what?"

"I've been back at the gym for months."

"You have?"

"I didn't tell you," he said, "because I didn't want you to make a big deal about it."

"Good call," I said. "Because I would have."

He stared at the ceiling.

"The thing is," he said, "boxing didn't seem to fit in. Not once I came out. I didn't expect that people would treat me differently. But they did. The girls at school were suddenly desperate to be my friend. *Ooh, Cam, let's go to the mall. Ooh, Cam, do my makeup.* It's not that I didn't want to do those things—I loved every glorious minute of it. It just seemed to overshadow everything else. Even some of the teachers jumped on the Cam bandwagon. *Oh, Cam, could you write about your experience as a gay teen for the school newspaper? Oh, Cam, we need someone with flair to decorate the gym for the dance.* People expected me to act a certain way, so I did. I let a side of myself slip away. I didn't mean to—it just happened."

I knew what he meant. I'd spent months slipping away too.

"That photo we took yesterday?" he said. "I posted it on Instagram. I captioned it *Coming Out*."

I smiled. "I like that."

"What will you do with your photos?" he asked.

"Lewis and I uploaded them to a pinup thread on Reddit."

He raised an eyebrow. "People might say mean things."

I shrugged. "They might say good things too."

He leaned over, kissed my nose.

"Cam?"

"Yeah?"

"I'm sorry for being so selfish all the time. You were right; it's not always about me."

He smiled. "Don't worry, Pops, I'm used to you being my"—he paused for effect—"narcis-sister."

I laughed. "Good one."

He reached out, moved a strand of hair from my face. "I'm glad we made up. I hate it when things are tense between us."

"Me too," I said. "It's so"—I paused for effect—"unsibilized."

He groaned in defeat. "Damn you, Poppy."

I inched closer to him. My heart fluttered at the thought of life without him.

But that would never happen.

There was a big layer of superglue between us now.

I thought of what happened in the back room at Bliss.

"Cam?" I said. "Will you be okay?"

His face was sad but hopeful. "I don't know. Maybe. I think so?"

I looked into his eyes. "Say something funny, Cam."

"I've been reading the thesaurus lately," he said, "because a mind is a terrible thing to garbage."

He reached for my pinkie. "Do you remember our very first pinkie promise?"

I smiled. "It was in the womb. You punched through your amniotic sac and into mine and you grabbed my teeny-tiny baby finger and promised to love me forever."

"Yes," he said. "I remember it clearly."

The End

ACKNOWLEDGMENTS

Feedback was vital to the writing of this book. Special thanks to Nicolas Martinez—for your honesty, your openness, and your enthusiasm. Thanks also to fellow author Robin Stevenson, and to my roller derby go-to girl Kelly Fry (aka Vex Murphy).

Many thanks to the Canada Council for the Arts. Your generous funding is much appreciated.

As always, a tip of the hat to my agent, Amy Tompkins. Your guidance is invaluable.

Last, but not least, heartfelt thanks to Lynne Missen and Peter Phillips. Your keen insights strengthen my writing. I am grateful.

Don't miss

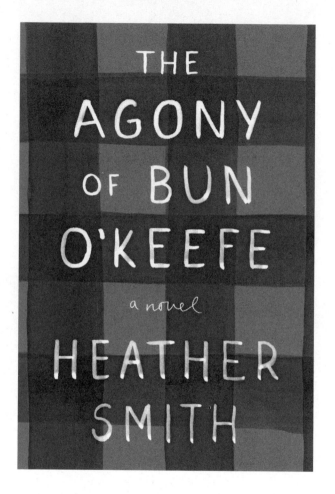

THE
AGONY
OF BUN
O'KEEFE
a novel
HEATHER
SMITH

Winner of the Ruth and Sylvia Schwartz Children's Book Award

Shortlisted for the OLA White Pine Award, the Amy Mathers Teen
Book Award, and the Geoffrey Bilson Award for Historical Fiction

A Kirkus Reviews Best Teen Book of 2017

It's Newfoundland, 1986. Fourteen-year-old Bun O'Keefe has lived a solitary life in an unsafe, unsanitary house. Her mother is a compulsive hoarder, and Bun has had little contact with the outside world. What she's learned about life comes from the random books and old VHS tapes that she finds in the boxes and bags her mother brings home. Bun and her mother rarely talk, so when Bun's mother tells Bun to leave one day, she does.

Hitchhiking out of town, Bun ends up on the streets of St. John's. Fortunately, the first person she meets is Busker Boy, a street musician who senses her naivety and takes her in. Together they live in a house with an eclectic cast of characters: Chef, a hotel dishwasher with culinary dreams; Cher, a drag queen with a tragic past; Big Eyes, a Catholic school girl desperately trying to reinvent herself; and The Landlord, a man whom Bun is told to avoid at all cost.

Through her experiences with her new roommates, and their sometimes tragic revelations, Bun learns about the world beyond the walls of her mother's house and discovers the joy of being part of a new family.

Read on for an excerpt . . .

CHAPTER ONE

She yelled, "Go on! Get out!" So I did. It wasn't easy. The path to the door was filled in again. I tried to keep it clear. But it was like shoveling in a snowstorm. There was only so much I could pile up on either side before it started caving in again. Not that I left the house much.

At one point I had to turn sideways and suck in. I wondered how she did it. She was over three hundred pounds. As I inched forward I saw frozen smiles through a clear plastic bin. Barbie Dolls, $10 As Is.

I knew without looking there'd be some without limbs.

I tripped on a lamp and fell on a bike. She didn't even laugh. The only sound was the tick-tick-tick of the bike's spinning wheel. I watched till it slowed to a stop.

I took one last look at her before I disappeared behind a mountain of junk. She was nestled into a pile of garbage bags, a cup of tea balanced on her chest, and I wondered, how will she get up without me?

Boxes and bags lined the walls. As I squeezed down

the hall I said *therianthropy* over and over 'cause I liked the way it bounced in my mouth. It was one of the words I said out loud when I hadn't used my voice in a while. It meant "having the power to turn into an animal." I'd read it in an old anthropology textbook and I thought, Wouldn't it be nice if my mother could turn herself into a humming-bird? That way she could flit in and out through the piles of junk that filled every nook and cranny of the house. It was a nice thought, her being a shape-shifter. Maybe, I decided, that's how I should remember her.

~

I walked down our laneway with my arms crossed over my chest. I had forgotten my jacket. I wouldn't go back for it. Not after the trouble it took me to get out.

I counted Mississippis down the long gravel road. By the time I reached the highway I'd had two coughing fits. She did the trek every day. An empty wagon on the way into town, a full one on the way back. I figured she had exceptional lungs.

At the main road I stuck out my thumb. What I knew about hitchhiking came from *The Texas Chain Saw Massacre*. It came home in a box of VHS tapes. When I told her we didn't have a player she said, "There she goes, never satisfied, always asking for more." When I pointed out that I had asked for nothing and was simply stating a fact, she didn't talk to me for days. Months later a VHS player showed up and I popped in the tape. I watched it on the floor model TV she'd pulled home on a wooden toboggan. It had a missing button so I had to change the channel with a pair of pliers. The screen had fuzzy lines going through it, which made the movie even scarier. The hitchhiker wanted to kill people. I had no intentions of killing anyone so I figured there was no harm in sticking out my thumb on the main road.

I went to St. John's. Seemed as good a place as any. Only two hours away and easy to disappear into.

~

I figured there were places for people like me, people whose mother said, "Go on! Get out!" After all, there were places for people like Jimmy Quinlan. He was in the box with *The Texas Chain Saw Massacre*. He drank too much alcohol and lived on the streets of Montreal. Just one of the many "derelict human beings in Canada—living their lives around a bottle of cheap wine, rubbing alcohol or even, on a bad day, aftershave lotion."

I watched the documentary so much I'd memorized the script. Alone in the house I'd recite it. Sometimes I'd say *aftershave lotion*, over and over, putting the emphasis on *shave*, just as the narrator had. I'd copy his gravelly voice too. I'd say, "Quinlan's nerves are raw," till I wasn't me anymore; I was a faceless man in the TV.

I walked along Duckworth Street and asked the first person that looked like they might know. I waited till he finished his song.

"Any missions around here?"

"Missions?"

"Yes. Where alcoholics with no homes go."

He smiled. "You're an alcoholic, are you?"

"No. But I have no home."

"Sorry. I don't know of any missions."

"Are you sure?"

"I'm sure."

I must have looked doubtful 'cause he said, "Why are you asking *me*? Do I look like a homeless alcoholic?"

He looked nothing like Jimmy Quinlan or the other derelict human beings. For one thing, he had teeth. But he *was* begging, which is what Jimmy Quinlan did within the first two minutes of the film. He stopped cars and people on the busy streets. *"Bonjour, monsieur! Bonjour, monsieur!"*

"You look like a normal person," I said. "But you *are* begging."

He gathered the loose change from the guitar case in front of him. "I'm not begging. I'm busking."

"So you have a home?"

"I never said that."

"So you *don't* have a home."

He fit his guitar into the guitar-shaped space and squinted at me. "Who are you?"

"Bun O'Keefe."

He snapped the lid shut and hopped to his feet.

"First time in the city?"

"Yes."

"How did you get here?"

"Hitchhiked."

"You shouldn't do that."

"Why not? I wasn't going to murder anyone."

He gave me a funny look and headed down a steep hill toward the harbor. He didn't say good-bye so I followed. When he went into a coffee shop, I stood behind him in line, and the girl behind the counter said, "You two together?" and I said, "Yes."